MW01535501

Desperate TO FORGET

Desperate
TO
FORGET

Vanessa Holliday

gatekeeper press
Columbus, Ohio

DESPERATE TO FORGET

Published by **Gatekeeper Press**
2167 Stringtown Rd, Suite 109
Columbus, OH 43123-2989
www.GatekeeperPress.com

Library of Congress Control Number: 2021953278

ISBN (hardcover): 9781662920592
ISBN (paperback): 9781662912344
eISBN: 9781662922275

For Tim

1

"DRAMA THIS AND SOAP OPERA GAG ME THAT."

The noise is what woke her.

She sat up and rubbed the sleepy from her eyes. She reached for Bosco, her pig with soft stuffing and a missing ear. She approached the window and watched harsh wind rip tree branches from their resting place. Leaves danced violently across the lawn, foreboding a storm. The scene sketched itself into her memory.

It was reasonable to believe the noise downstairs was her parents. It was the a.m. of her sixth birthday, and the possibility of her plea for a dollhouse being assembled enticed her to go spy on them.

Careful not to let the floorboards squeak beneath her, she placed a socked foot on the wooden stair. She nearly giggled because she got to the bottom without a sound.

Clutching Bosco to her chest, she peeked around the archway into the living room.

Two unfamiliar dark figures shifted in the black.

She froze with paralyzing fear.

In a matter of seconds one of them had his harsh grip on her nightgown and a hand over her mouth.

It was so cold.

Her stomach was so cold.

He pulled the blade from her.

"Dani?"

The light overpowered the dark. Her skin prickled to life and a choir of birds enveloped her ears. Though her eyelids were sealed, she visualized her grandmother's petite figure hovering over her with wrinkles of wisdom framing her olive irises.

Dani opened her eyes. The house was quiet, and no one was poised over her. She touched her toes to hardwood floor and noticed parchment with edges of a floral design taped to her door. It was a note her grandmother left.

It read: *Off to the grocery store. From your incoherent mumbling in your sleep, I surmised you have little food demands. Wish you the best of luck on day uno. May you meet a handsome fellow with the heart of a saint. - Agnes.*

"Ugh." She ripped the paper down and let it fall.

She showered and slid on her work uniform. The illustration of black slacks and black button-down branded her a bank robber. Her cousin Clare had gotten her this job. She wasn't sure if she was thankful yet.

She closed her bedroom door and descended the stairs of her grandmother's colonial in Riftin's downtown historical district. The two-story symmetrical square had a spiral staircase as its prominent feature. It spiraled below a vaulted ceiling with a chandelier that weighed a thousand cows. Agnes's words.

She drifted toward the kitchen for something to soothe the acid in her stomach. After she settled at the bar, the doorbell sounded. "Open!"

Her friend Hazel appeared in the doorway. Every strand of her long brunette hair was perfectly in place, and her lithe body was encased in a small fortune of designer labels. She held up a flawlessly manicured finger, those of her other hand pecking her cell phone. She landed on a bar stool with a pensive look on her face. "The douche was texting."

Problematic testosterone as standard procedure it appeared. "What douche?"

"Xavier." Her friend's fingers found her hair and twisted it as she always did when life didn't suit her. "I saw him at the mall with his tongue down a girl's throat, so I dumped his two-timing ass. Now he wants me back. Swore it was a one-time slip up."

"Mmm-hmm."

Hazel huffed. "I thought we had something."

"Screw him."

"I don't know." She already backpedaled. "He's pretty hot."

Good old Hazel . . . shallow as a dinner plate.

"He was perfect," she reminisced.

"Perfect?" Dani dropped her spoon in the bowl. "He was arrogant, rude, and had the mental capacity of a goldfish."

"Why do I bother talking to you?"

Something the person sitting next to her would like to know also. "You should set your sights higher. And by higher, I'm referring to morality, not attractiveness."

"A classic manhunt," she said with a mischievous wink. "I like it."

Dani tossed her cereal bowl in the sink. "Whatever. I need my ride now."

On the drive Hazel picked apart Xavier's inadequacies as a man while Dani assured her with the usual broken record of sentences. Hazel dated and discarded so many losers, Dani didn't tire her brain keeping up anymore. She had dated none herself to share this loveless torment of hers. She was nineteen and had never dated. Guys asked her out, but she had acquired the forte of slyly easing away with creative excuses that originated from the depths of her imaginative brain. Anything bested an evening with a debauchee who expected "action," as Hazel often called it, at its closure.

She rolled down the window to get some fresh air and muffle the damsel in distress. Hazel didn't seem to mind. She had already drifted into another dimension, letting anger and self-pity get the best of her.

When they arrived at the restaurant Hazel patted Dani on the back like a mother sending her child off to kindergarten. "Remember, dear one. Steak reeks less than fish."

"Thank you. Your pointless parlance does nothing for me in the slightest." Dani exited the vehicle and stared at her new second home. The steakhouse was stoned and landscaped, intended to impress the public eye.

There was little expectation this job would turn out better than her first. If history repeated itself, the foul seafood smell, rude customers, or the occasional mop of bodily fluids wouldn't drive her to quit. It would be a single person.

She approached the front door and swung it open to reveal the interior. What lay within Steak Grate was an elaborate fortress. Gigantic brass light fixtures, modern abstract paintings, and detailed woodwork set the stage for absurd.

She walked to the cash register and scanned for any sign of life. She realized she couldn't remember her boss's name.

"Hello."

Dani turned around.

"Liza, in case you forgot."

"I didn't," she lied.

"You excited?"

"Sure," she lied twice.

She was in chafing clothing and being forced to stand on her feet for hours for pathetic pay. Yes, "excited" was the word *du jour*.

* * *

Ian ducked his head to dodge flying onion rings. "Piss off!"

Travis's head rocked back with laughter and ruthlessly threw another toy of torture.

"Don't you throw another damn one!"

Travis's expression was that of a five-year-old being threatened not to do something, but knowing deep in his heart he's going to do it anyway. He threw another onion ring that smacked Ian in the neck.

"That's it!" Ian let go of the tea pitchers and tackled Travis to the ground. Kitchenware flew in every direction. Other servers afforded them a glance, but only a brief one. This kind of thing was a common occurrence around here.

"You don't like onions?" Travis quipped.

Satisfied Ian had inflicted a bruise or two, he rose off the irritant.

The kitchen manager passed through while Travis shamelessly picked floor debris off his uniform. Brent cocked an eyebrow. "Should I ask?"

"I'd rather you didn't." Ian bolted out the double doors. He needed a cigarette.

He rounded the corner and froze into place. The new girl was standing next to Liza at the cash register.

"Damn," Travis stole the word from Ian's thinking. "She is fine. Dibs." And Travis marched toward her in demonstration.

"Fine" only brushed the surface. The girl was gorgeous.

"Hey, stud," Rebecca greeted, startling Ian to the core.

His attempt to avoid his relentless stalker was futile. He wondered when Travis would get sick of her like he was. "Hey."

"Me and some friends are thinking about having a party . . ." Her voice trailed off because Ian stopped listening.

Eventually everything fell quiet. He looked at her and she eagerly waited for an answer to a question he paid little attention to. "No thanks?" was always his default response, and then his cue to escape.

* * *

The training process evolved into the repetition of idiot-proof tasks like Dani was an inept dumbass. Why people sized her up as five IQ points higher than a doorknob was an unanswered anomaly. "Yeah. I think I got it."

"I'll let you wait tables soon, but I'm short a cashier right now. And you don't have to answer the phone."

Because that was set aside for the inventor of the lightbulb and other geniuses.

A brown-haired boy suddenly caught her off guard. Without missing a beat, he extended his hand and accosted her. "Hi, there. I'm Travis."

Out of her peripheral she noticed Liza fold her arms, but he either ignored it or didn't care. Probably the second.

"This is Dani," Liza spoke for her. "Anything else we can do for you?"

He put his hand back down. "Dani. Pretty. Is that short for Danielle?"

"No," Dani finally spoke.

"What are you doing over here? Don't you need to be rolling silverware?" Liza interrogated.

"I'm just being friendly." His stare reminded Dani of a starving, salivating carnivore.

Gross.

Liza's heel closed the money safe underneath. "Well, come get me if you need anything. I'm unlocking the doors."

To Dani's delight, Travis left too. "And if you need anything from me. . ."

She most certainly would not.

The second Liza unlocked the doors, Dani's mind drifted to something from a zombie film. A massive plague outbreak hits once-civilized cities now masked with overgrown vines of vegetation. She imagined a stampede of zombies with intense hunger in their rotted eyes.

There was no horde. What served in its place was an elderly couple already complaining about the cold temperature inside.

Liza sauntered past the desk and eyed each key chained to her belt. Her bleached hair flopped behind her.

Dani adjusted her uniform, turned the toothpick dispenser ninety degrees, gathered the pens scattered on the counter, and stacked menus in a neater pile. After she devoted too much time doing this, she feared being obsessive-compulsive and stopped.

She spotted Travis wave at her from across the restaurant. Her eyes shifted to the person next to him.

She was highly alarmed becoming mesmerized with the kinetic energy of straws being crammed down an apron. The apron was tied tightly around an artfully sculpted subject with black spiked hair. He turned toward her and revealed the ultimate perfection of a face.

Sweat crystallized on her palms and her tongue swelled in the back of her throat.

Did she have the flu?

Travis chatted in the point-of-interest's ear while they waited for customers to arrive. Their aprons unveiled their identities as waiters.

When nighttime fell, Travis, as predicted, hindered her departure with an offer of a ride she would never take and an invitation to a party she would never go to.

Hazel picked her up as promised, but by the time she shifted the conversation topic away from Xavier, Dani's ear was already violated.

"Anything interesting happen at work?" her friend quizzed.

They entered the dying business of a movie rental store, probably the last one in existence. It was a sad old thing with flickering fluorescent lights, tired shelving, and the smell of dust and rancid carpet.

"Since when is babysitting the public interesting?" Dani finally answered.

"Any hot guys work there?"

"A weird question." She knew better than to mention the waiter. Hazel would never shut up about it. Ever. "But I'll have my eyes peeled for your next philanderer."

Hazel always gave her the same look when she was annoyed with her. It was like she found a bug in her soup, thoroughly revolted and inconvenienced.

"Whoops. Slipped out."

"What the hell is a philanderer?" Hazel bitched.

"Men who defile women absent of qualm."

"Qualm?"

"Do you ever read a book?"

"No, I'm normal. Reading encyclopedias is what freaks do. One minute you're flipping pages, the next you're rocking yourself talking to a convection oven."

Dani wistfully looked over at the documentary section.

"Don't even think about it," Hazel warned with a finger. "Nothing boring."

"As opposed to your selection. Drama this and soap opera gag me that."

"Documentaries are for people with canes and upcoming cataract surgery." Her friend held up a movie. The cover was different shades of pink with a couple embracing. "What about this one?"

Dani looked up at the ceiling. "Where's a noose so I can hang myself?"

2

"THIS IS HOW THE HORROR MOVIES START."

"That new girl, she's so hot," Travis chanted for the fiftieth time.

"Yea, I got that. Can you shut up about it now?" Ian was propped up against the wall with his arms folded across his chest, irritated as usual.

The rain picked up momentum outside and pounded harshly on the metal roof above them. The sky exploded with multiple lightning bolts, and pockets of thunder popped with ear-piercing cracks. It took him a moment to recognize her through the window. Despite the weather, the new cashier was walking in slow strides while everyone else ran for shelter like there was no tomorrow. "You're dating Rebecca, you jackass."

"Well, not really."

"Just banging her then. Chivalrous."

"Dude. I bet she looks smoking in a bikini."

Ian craned his neck and looked at him. "I can't listen to you anymore." Eager to slip away from him, he headed for the register.

She was counting money when he closed the distance. Her natural dirty blonde hair was wet from the storm. "Fun in the rain?"

She looked up but didn't say anything.

He cleared his throat. "Got a pen?"

She stoically placed a cup of pens on the counter.

"Alright." He fingered through the writing utensils and scribbled with one to make sure it worked, but mostly stalling for time. He smiled. "Thanks. I'm Ian Price by the way."

No smile was returned to him. She resumed counting the bills in her hand.

He refused to walk away. "Now tell me your name."

She looked up, her face pinched with annoyance. "Why the hell do you want my name?"

What the shit.

He kept his feet planted to the place in front of her. They both stared at each other, neither of them blinking.

Liza passed him to unlock the doors and let in the promise of whining patrons. "Ian, position."

With that, he backed up and walked away.

* * *

On the second workday, the same Rebecca girl manned the hostess podium. Dani didn't envy her. Customers always rejected the first offer of a seat. She had suffered through that aneurism-worthy task before.

"Can we sit by a window?"

"We'd like a booth."

"We need a larger table."

"It's too loud over here."

"Yeah, this ain't happening."

Like where they sat was life or death to them. People are starving all over the world, but these people couldn't eat unless their ass cheeks were mashed against booth cushions in perfect coordinates.

"Where's the restroom?" Someone had come up to the counter.

Dani robotically pointed. As the woman hurried away like her bladder was three seconds from exploding, the phone rang its fourth ring.

Rebecca glared at her from across the way. "You going to answer it or stare at it like a retard?"

It would be highly unnecessary to conduct an analysis to classify the hostess into its correct phylum. Rebecca was a hateful bitch.

She yanked up the phone. "Steak Grate. How can I help you?"

"Umm . . . yeah . . . I need to order something." The caller was nearly inaudible.

She looked around for a pad and pen. "Go ahead."

"What you got?"

She looked under the counter and plucked up a menu.

"Hello?" prompted the man on the phone.

"Yes, sir. Our dinners are rack of ribs, sirloin—"

"Yea, I'll have that sirloin."

She wrote that down.

"I want it medium-well."

She wrote that down too.

"Actually, make it medium-rare."

She scratched out her previous.

"Don't I get two sides?"

"Yes, sir. What would you like?"

"What you got?"

She searched for side orders. "Cajun fries, baked potato, asparagus—"

"Umm . . . hold on a sec. Honey, what side you want? Ok, yeah. Can you read those off again so my wife can hear? She's deaf as a post."

"Cajun fries, baked potato, asparagus, Caesar salad—"

"Alright, she wants a loaded baked potato, extra sour cream, lots of sour cream. How much is an extra side?"

"$6.45."

"Forget that then."

"Anything else, sir?"

"Umm . . . hold on. Honey, you want something else? Nah, we're good. How much is two of those?"

She calculated it in her head. "$59.90 plus tax."

"Good gracious! You got chicken?" Then he coughed so loud in her ear it felt like her eardrum burst.

"$17.95."

"Where do you get off charging people that kind of money? I'm taking my business elsewhere."

Click.

"Someone shoot me." She hung up the phone already out of mental deodorant for the day. For the week. No, month.

A half hour shy of closing time, Liza appeared at the counter. "I need you to get paper towel boxes from my car. They aren't heavy."

"No problem."

Liza fished in her pocket for the keys. "It's a white minivan, upper parking lot."

It was a long walk then.

Liza caught Dani's worried flush, but she slammed the keys down and walked off anyway. Such a classy broad, that one.

It provided little comfort that the adjacent shops outside were closed and lifeless. Liza's lack of foresight this was dangerous for a young woman perturbed her. She walked up the paved hill and heard the chronic buzz of overhead signs above her. "This is how the horror movies start."

She browsed through the cars and espied a white van. She unlocked it and climbed in. Her boss needed to do a serious cleanup because the smell of rotten food curled her nose hairs and her sneakers stuck to the floor.

She went straight for the boxes. "They aren't heavy, my ass."

She climbed out with the cargo, locked the door with her elbow, and shut the door with her hip. She tightened her grip on the boxes as she walked with partial vision.

Her heart skipped a beat at footsteps behind her.

No. It was just her nerves.

A man in tattered clothing darted in front of her. "What's the hurry, honey?" He made a sick sound with his mouth like he was slurping through a straw.

She let go of the boxes and clenched her fist. "Get away from me."

He slapped her to the pavement.

She backed up on her palms and ran.

When she realized no one was behind her, she looked back. Her eyes widened at the sight of two men in a brawl behind her.

When she reached the gas station it was difficult to communicate without enough oxygen in her lungs for the attendant to call the police. The man nodded and informed the operator. After providing the necessary details, he hung up and asked if she was ok.

She gave him a thumbs up. Still in hyperventilation mode, she sank down to the floor and used a shelf as a back prop. She felt her heart pulsing through her neck and wondered if it would ever calm down again. She touched her cheek. There was a gash and she was bleeding.

The wail of sirens got closer, so she pushed herself off the floor. As she neared, the flash of chaotic blue lights blinded her. She scanned the vehicles and saw the scumbag wedged in a back seat. She breathed in relief and walked to the men in uniform.

She froze.

"This is her," Ian informed them.

"Hello ma'am. Officer Quade. Are ya alright?"

The policeman was not a pretty sight to beholder. Quade had a pot belly, poor coloring in his face, and spoke with an accent that was as Southern as humanly possible. Though that part was endearing.

"I'm fine, sir."

After a firm shake of the officer's hand, Ian made his way back to the restaurant.

Her first question. "Is that man alright?"

"Man?"

"Yeah. The one that dipshit was fighting."

"The only person harmed was your attacker." Quade pointed behind him. "That boy fought 'em off."

Dani looked past the policeman. She watched Ian disappear around the building. He had no injuries, no cuts, no signs of a struggle taking place.

"We need to ask a few questions and then we'll take ya to the clinic and get ya cleaned up. Why were ya out here?"

"My boss asked me to get . . ." She spotted the cardboard boxes where she'd abandoned them. "Paper towels from her van."

Quade put his pad away after he was done questioning her. "That's a nasty cut ya got. Ya need to go to the clinic and get that disinfected and stitched."

"Nah, I'm alright."

"I don't think so. Looks like somethin' sharp got ya. Might've been wearin' a ring."

"Yeah, well. I don't have a car. Mine's in the shop."

"I'll take ya. I'm headin' that way and my buddy here is takin' that gentleman to jail."

It was a weird thought being in the back seat of a cop car. "Are you sure?"

"Yeah."

She followed him. "This should be interesting."

After settling in, she realized there was no handle from the inside, the officer and criminal were separated by glass, and there was no leg room whatsoever.

"Comfortable?"

"Not, at, all."

He laughed.

3

"NINJA SCHOOL, THE USUAL MARTIAL ARTS TRAINING?"

After checking in at the clinic, she washed up the best she could in the bathroom and claimed a seat in the lobby. Looking at magazines to pass the time wasn't really an option. It wasn't necessarily because the crinkled photo paper was covered in snot; she'd just rather read about something other than fake diet remedies and health scares.

Since time was all she had, she profiled its inhabitants. There was a tanned woman with a sleepy child in her lap. A few seats over, a younger man had passed out on a stiff-looking couch but didn't seem to mind. An elderly woman was snug in the corner with the magazine racks. She hummed while she flipped through one.

That left the woman next to her, who was coughing and hacking into a handkerchief that was no longer white.

Dani looked across the room and saw a box of tissues. She got up and handed them to her.

The sick woman peered up at her with the most sleep-deprived eyes in the world. Her hair was a beautiful shade of red but hadn't seen shampoo in a couple of days. She motioned toward her ear and indicated she was deaf.

Dani signed, *I know sign.*

The woman's face lit up. She signed her name. *Ella.*

Dani.

What do you do?

College. You?

Before deaf, prison guard.

Interesting.

Prisoner stabbed ear. Infection took both.

Sorry.

Ella blew her nose into Dani's offering. *I forgive him. Met husband at deaf center. All God's plan. Worst thing got me here.*

"Miss Poe?"

Dani stood up and looked at the deaf woman. *Feel better.*

After a long wait, an unfriendly nurse harshly stitched her mandible flesh back together. "These are dissolvable so don't come back."

Gosh darn. And here she was enjoying the pleasure of her company.

"Hey."

Dani was surprised to see Ian in her doorway.

"Can I come in?" he asked politely but entered the room anyway. He leaned down while the nurse put her bandage on. Well, slapped it to her face, rather.

He was so close she could see his hair shine in the florescent light. His dark eyes matched his hair and leather jacket. There was something ominous about the way he looked.

The nurse straightened and gaped at him for a few seconds too long. She turned to Dani with envy in her eyes.

"As fun as this has been, I think I'll get out of here now." Dani jumped off the bed and went to the front desk.

Ian followed her. "I thought you might need a lift home."

She quickened her pace. "No, no. I got it covered." The idea of being alone with him did something to her insides.

She signed out at the nurse's station and used their phone to dial home. She would have called Hazel if she actually knew her number.

She glanced at the wall clock after a few rings. Agnes was likely in bed wearing earplugs. Due to Dani's loud video games, her grandmother had resorted to blocking out gunfire with foam shoved in her ear canal.

She noticed Ian out of the corner of her eye. He had stuck around. His back was propped against the wall, his hands pocketed in torn, faded jeans. He was this alpha male, light as a feather like no guilt could weigh him down. He put all the girls' hearts through a blender while he didn't possess a worry in the world. He was an exact replica of every guy Hazel had ever dated. Thus, any good in him was an illusion.

He started to smile.

The phone rang in her ear at least fifteen times before she gave up.

Now he was looking at her. "Offer still stands."

She didn't have a ton of options at this point. "Do you mind?"

He pushed himself off the wall and she reluctantly followed. Her eyes traced the back of his messy black hair. "So, where were you stationed exactly? Ninja school, the usual martial arts training?"

He decided to play along. "Where else?"

"Where did you learn to fight like that?"

"I'm a ninja. I thought we covered this."

She couldn't help but address the elephant. "Why did you help me?"

"What was I supposed to do? Walk away and whistle?"

27

The elevator door closed, and the sounds of ridiculous elevator music followed them down. She examined his body for any sign of injury. He caught her staring, so she immediately stopped.

The elevator dinged on the correct floor, and they walked out into the parking garage. He suddenly stopped in front of a motorcycle and tossed her a helmet.

"Umm. . ."

"You got a problem?"

"When you said a ride, I envisioned four tires."

"You don't strike me as the kind of person that scares easily."

"I'm not scared to die. It's just how I'm reconsidering."

He placed the helmet on her head anyway and tightened the strap. The palm of his hand brushed against her neck. "Don't be a wimp."

"Uh, thanks?" she stammered through a constricted throat, which again made her wonder if she had the flu.

She took her place on the bike behind him. Her arms wrapped around his waist, and she instantly felt hard muscle. She inhaled the scent of intoxicating redolence. He smelled of soap, tobacco, and motor oil. It sounded terrible. It wasn't.

He ripped forward to the street. While coasting through a hazy blur, she enjoyed the sensation of sandpaper wind on her face.

With shouted directions, he pulled his motorcycle up to the curb of her house. She wobbled off and regained her balance. The violent vibrations had briefly hindered her ability to stand. She removed the helmet and shook her hair out while he watched her with an unreadable expression on his face.

"You enjoyed that, didn't you?"

"No," she resisted and gave him his helmet.

He reached in his pocket and handed her something. It was her cell phone. "I snagged it from the restaurant. Hope you don't mind."

Even though it seemed harmless, she wondered if he withheld it deliberately. "I could have used this earlier."

"Could have. But then I wouldn't have your arms wrapped around me."

Her face felt hot.

"Stay safe, Dani." He rode off into the night. The roar of the engine faded into the black, as did red luminous tail lights.

While she stood there on the lawn in the company of crickets, there was a hollowing in the pit of her stomach. It was like something was missing, as if the man on the motorcycle had taken it with him.

* * *

Nathan Greer remembered the smell. It was the smell of burnt flesh in the rubble. He coughed, then yanked a cloth from his pocket to cover his nose. "My God."

"I told you to put rub under your nose." Kessler stepped up next to him, having none of it on himself. He was wearing a classic brown suit and tie just like all the classic detectives wore.

"You didn't."

"I'm used to it. You're not."

He was right. It was only his third crime scene. The first two were a house burglary and a convenience store robbery, and no one was hurt. All the training at the academy and writing traffic violations had not prepared him for this.

"What do you see?" Kessler asked.

Greer looked around. "Arson."

Kessler should have been annoyed by the simplicity of his answer. He wasn't. "The bodies?"

He reluctantly inched toward the remains. It was a husband and wife. He couldn't help but think about his own wife. That part about not internalizing—having a healthy separation between yourself and the victim—he had not mastered that.

"Greer?"

He leaned forward. "Stab wounds to the woman."

"The man?"

It took him a moment. "Gunshot?"

Kessler leaned down with him. "Where do you see an entry wound?"

"I don't."

"It's because it's not there."

He looked at his superior, relieved to look away from the dead for a minute.

Kessler pointed it out. "Strangulation."

He strained to look where his partner was pointing. It was the remnants of a windpipe. He suddenly felt like he was going to vomit. He stood up and walked out of the yellow-taped perimeter.

Kessler followed him, unfazed, with a cup of coffee in his hand. "You said you wanted to investigate homicides."

"I'm sorry." He was beyond embarrassed but there wasn't anything he could do about it. If he had stayed one more second, he would have puked in the crime scene. The fresh air was helping him forget the atrocious smell.

"Don't be sorry, kid. We're all like this at first."

"No, you're not. You're just trying to make me feel better."

"Nah. Some just hide it better than others."

Greer looked over his shoulder. "What about the girl?"

"She's in ICU. Stab wound to the stomach. She went through surgery but hasn't woken up yet."

"Talking to her will be critical. We might get lucky and she saw their face."

Kessler took a sip from his Styrofoam coffee cup. "Maybe."

"How old is she?"

For the first time since they arrived his colleague looked uncomfortable. "She's six."

4

"FROM A MACARONI
AND CHEESE BOX."

Dani waited for an eternity behind a woman with acute difficulty finalizing her syrup choice.

With her eye now twitching, she stepped up to the counter and ordered a shot of espresso. She selected cinnamon from the elegant array of stainless-steel canisters and sprinkled it before downing the brew. As the liquid started to burn her throat someone tapped her on the shoulder.

Hazel was barely recognizable. Her outfit was salmon-colored pants and a shirt two sizes too big. A bird's nest of hair, ugly glasses, and smeared lipstick marred the identity of her visage. "Hazel?"

She smiled. In addition to her other attributes, she had stained her teeth orange. "I have the most brilliant idea."

"I don't want to know about it."

"This is my chance to weed out the shallow guys. Only guys nice to me today when I'm ugly get to be potential husbands." Hazel flipped her uncombed hair for effect.

Dani glanced at the time on her phone. "I'm meeting your crazy ass in the lobby after?"

"I need to add some more orange to my teeth." To Dani's amazement, Hazel plucked out a zip lock bag of orange powder. Before she departed, she said, "From a macaroni and cheese box. I'm a genius."

She watched her friend disappear while other students snickered behind her back.

After four flights of stairs and a pointless class later, she found Hazel at the center table in the lobby under the oxeye window with a surplus of revulsion on her face.

Dani plopped down in a chair. "So. How'd it go?"

Hazel swatted at something in the air. "Oh, just aces. My experiment is a failure!"

"You don't say."

*   *   *

The rumble of a diesel engine and the squeal of eighteen tires greeted her. The men in uniform with beer guts and untrimmed beards jumped down.

One of them belched. "Let's get in, get out."

They marched to the back of the truck and lifted chained metal. A formed assembly line took each cardboard cube to the back storeroom of the restaurant.

"Aren't you early, Dani?" Liza appeared wearing her ugly mustard polo. "I need you to help me with something."

Dani's theory was Liza skipped over feelings of guilt about sending her to her possible death. She wasn't expecting fireworks after being slapped around by a thug, but her boss withholding an apology even took her by surprise. History repeats itself.

One of the delivery men shoved a clipboard at Liza. She signed it and handed it back without looking at it. "I need a minute." She

34

gestured toward her boyfriend. "Can you wait for me out here?" She disappeared without Dani's consent.

This must be the boyfriend she had been dating for five years, but he was too much of a baby to marry her. Or at least that was the news that propelled through the grapevine of useless information.

Dani noticed the kitchen manager at an iron table where employees chain smoked. Brent defined intimidating. His skin looked about forty-five years old and was marked with elaborate tattoo sleeves on each arm. His muscular figure and shaved head added to the edgy persona. She timidly approached and wondered if he was as mean as he looked.

He wasn't.

"Hey," Brent said softly.

"Hey. We haven't officially met."

"You're Dani. The girl that bastard bothered."

"And you're Brent. Kitchen manager."

"Now we've met." He stomped his cigarette out and lit another methodically. "You alright?"

"Thanks to Ian. I guess."

"Yeah. Good kid," he volunteered.

For some reason she felt completely at ease with him. She sat at the table and didn't think twice about it. "What do you know about him?"

"Guy window shopping?"

"Since I don't know what that is, no."

"Well. He's been here since Liza opened the place. Him and Travis fight on occasion, but that's to be expected. Travis is a pest."

"Travis?" she asked uninterested at the new topic.

"Yeah. Cockier than a pro football player. Always causing trouble around here."

"Uh huh. Anything else?"

Smoke seemed to expel from his lungs in slow motion. "About Ian, you mean. Why don't you ask him yourself?"

Her eyes darted toward the metal door when it careened open. Liza had a guilty expression like she'd had frisky time in the broom closet. Whether she did or didn't, Dani didn't want to know about it.

Brent pulled the cigarette from his mouth. "Do us all a favor, Liza, and don't get her killed."

A pout spread across her makeup-caked face. The sunlight did wonders to make her resemble a clown. "Who do you think you're talking to? Get off your worthless ass and go scrub something."

He didn't bother with a rebuttal. He just stood up and headed back inside. There was something pitiful about it.

Liza walked off in the opposite direction. Her split personality took effect. "We need to get boxes from my car. It's so beautiful outside. How ethereal."

Dani wondered why the refined word was part of the woman's vocabulary. She probably snagged it from one of those romance novels with naked people on the cover. "Ethereal?"

"Yes," she boasted proudly. "It means—"

"I know what it means." The idea of someone as stupid as Liza giving her an English lesson made her skin crawl.

* * *

"I can't right now, Hazel."

"Why not?"

36

Dani stared at her gaming console. Her television lit up with her former comrades dying on a spectator camera. "I have influenza strand B. Pretty intense."

"You do not."

"Ebola virus."

"Come on, I need something for my date tomorrow," Hazel pleaded.

Dani hung up and tossed her cell on the couch.

"Really?"

She jumped. "Good grief, grandmother. You could have been an assassin."

"Dani?"

She sighed. "Need I justify a millionth time my disdain for jewelry and clothing emporiums?"

"Because AK-47s are more your style."

"You so get me."

Her grandmother inspected the shattered mess on the floor. "Is that a broken game controller?"

"Someone teabagged me."

Agnes held up her hands and left the room. "I'm going to pretend I don't know what that means."

The doorbell sounded and Dani peeked over the back side of the couch. "If that's Hazel, I'm going to slit my wrists."

"I'm not getting that!" her grandmother yelled.

Dani approached the window. "Why is Clare here?"

"Oh yeah. She needs help with wedding stuff."

"No." Her head hit the wall. "My off day is ruined."

It all started three weeks ago when Dani opened the front door for her cousin. Her long, platinum blonde hair was embellished with artificial daisies and braided down one side. Clare exclaimed in a loud decibel she was getting married. She talked at length about her fiancé Preston Tate, the wedding ceremony, the fabrics, the colors, the details of no interest. Then the moment arrived when she asked Dani to be a bridesmaid.

After Clare left, Agnes came outside on the porch to revisit Dani's decision. "Shouldn't we talk about this?"

"I know what you're thinking. I'm thinking the same. I would rather die than go back."

"Then why now? And for Clare, no less?"

"What Clare is or isn't doesn't interest me. I feel like there's something gnawing at me. I still don't sleep."

"Then you lied to me."

"You would harbor this incredible guilt if I didn't."

Her grandmother sat down on the porch swing. She stared at the grass with that same pathetic look on her face she always had. "I failed you."

"See, that's what I'm talking about. You never failed me. But for some reason you don't know that."

Agnes looked up at her. "I have to know."

She felt her chest tighten up. She knew what was coming.

"Are you using again?"

If Dani answered too quick or waited too long it would make her look guilty. "No."

* * *

One-seventy.

One-eighty.

One-ninety.

"Did you miss me?"

Dani averted her attention away from counting ten-dollar bills. Ian had propped himself against the counter unnoticed. "How's your day going?" he asked.

"I got to clean up a customer's vomit. It's swell."

A dimple tugged at the corner of his mouth. "I've had it better. I decked out a grille."

"A barbecue grill?"

"No. I work at Dax Auto on the side."

"Oh." She felt incredibly stupid for some reason.

When he shifted to one side, she noticed Rebecca watching them with a sour look on her face. It dawned on her that even though Rebecca was dating Travis, she probably had a thing for Ian.

"I'll leave you to it." He winked and walked off.

Out of the corner of her eye, she saw Agnes come in.

Oh no.

Dani came out from behind the counter. "Grandmother, Hi. What are you doing here?"

"I knew you wouldn't ask him. Even though you promised." She walked up to the hostess podium. "May I speak with Ian Price, please?"

Rebecca gave Dani a strange look. Dani's hand covered her eyes. Agnes had threatened to show up at the restaurant. Dani didn't think she would actually do it.

Rebecca did what she was asked and brought Ian to the front.

"Are you Ian Price?"

"Yes, ma'am."

"Hello. I'm Agnes, Dani's grandmother."

He shook her hand. "Pleasure."

"I'd like to invite you to lunch with us this week, to properly thank you. I knew Dani wouldn't have the courtesy to ask you."

He grinned. "Sounds great."

"Wonderful." Agnes turned around and gave Dani a dirty look before she left.

As a child Dani recited Shakespeare's sonnets on a stage without trepidation, but now her embarrassment was monumental. If the floor were a sinkhole, she would let it devour her.

Liza passed them. "Hey guys."

"Hey Liza." Dani and Ian replied in unison, both relieved for a distraction.

Liza stopped in her tracks and eyed them. They broke off in separate directions.

5

"I MAY OR MAY NOT STOLE THE DOG."

"Hey, sleepyhead."

"Ah!" Dani jerked and fell off the bed.

Hazel was propped up on all limbs like an insect. She collapsed from laughing so hard.

"I'm glad you're amused. Now get out."

"I'm here to make you beautiful."

Dani crawled back into her pillows. "No. Not happening."

"We don't have much time." Her friend hauled in a colossal box of endless beauty supplies that could last a woman a lifetime. "It's time for your makeover. I've been dying to do this for a while."

A deep regret of last night's text messages settled in. It had been a royal mistake telling Hazel about Agnes inviting Ian to lunch.

Hazel's arm pointed to a chair like a provoked schoolteacher followed by a snapping of her fingers. "Let's go. Wasting valuable time here."

"You're crazy if you think you're putting makeup on me."

"Dani, though your weirdness makes for interesting cups of coffee, it doesn't propel you in the romantic realm."

"If you're trying to insult me, you'll have to try harder."

There was a knock on the bedroom door and Agnes let herself in. "Dani, honey? Your date will be here in about thirty minutes. Do you need a shirt ironed?"

"I'm living in a nut house."

Hazel came over and rubbed her shoulder. "You're just nervous. We've all been there."

Dani shrugged her off. "Get off me."

"I remember being nervous for my first date," Agnes reminisced.

"Oh, me too. I about barfed," Hazel acceded.

Dani went over to her dresser drawers and pulled out some jeans and a white T-shirt while the pair relived their dating history. She left them upstairs because it didn't seem to matter if she was there or not.

After she changed, she decided to pass the time by sinking deeper into the living room sofa, fantasizing about it magically teleporting her to another dimension.

It wasn't long until Hazel and Agnes descended the stairs, chit-chatting about the most mundane of topics.

"Well, I tried." Hazel accepted defeat. "I've got to run, but I want details later."

"You got it." Agnes seemed amused as she shut the front door. "Did she ruffle your feathers, sweetheart?"

"Her. And you."

"It's raining. You know what they say. It's good luck."

"They also say it's good luck when a bird shits on you."

Agnes placed her hands on her hip. "Are you sure you want to wear *that* on a date?"

"Why do you keep calling it that? It's not a date. You're going to be there for crying out loud."

"Yes. Keep telling yourself that."

Dani straightened. "You're bailing, aren't you?"

"What was your first clue?"

"No! You can't do this to me!"

The doorbell dinged as if on cue. Her grandmother went to fetch it in a prissy manner.

Ian made his entrance in a sharp, blue button-down and ironed khakis. It was almost humorous to witness the charlatan personality. He was the gentleman every girl wanted to chauffeur to their parents, but secretly the troublemaker who snuck through their windows at night.

Agnes proceeded to thank him and rambled on about how brave he was, while he maintained his stature with nothing short of charming comments. The absence of any signs of nervousness made Dani want to smack him.

"You kids have a nice time." Agnes bid them farewell.

"Aren't you coming?" Ian asked.

"No, I'm not feeling well." And then she fake coughed to be an ass.

"Well, it was a pleasure seeing you again. Hope you feel better."

"Oh, I'm sure she will," Dani mumbled as she walked past them. She realized some fresh air would do her good, so she headed in that direction.

Outside she noticed a truck was substituted for his motorcycle. When they climbed in, there was a different scent about it. "You borrowed this?"

He settled in. "Yeah. It's Brent's."

"The kitchen manager?"

"That's the one." He cranked up. "Do you like Italian?"

"Whatever floats your boat." She folded her hands into each other and realized her palms were foamy from sweat and not the rain.

Did she really just say, 'whatever floats your boat?'

When they arrived, the building was extravagant stonework framed with wrought iron balconies, water fountains, and a yard landscaped by precise metacarpus. "The Blue Swan? People get married here and this is where we're eating?"

"Don't worry, I'm buying."

"No, you're not! I was supposed to—well—Agnes was before she ditched me."

He climbed out of the truck and opened the door for her regardless of her ranting. His finger touched her lips. It sent an instant ripple throughout her body. A breeze blew between them and induced his hair to stir in slower time. "Please just eat with me."

She sighed. "I'm paying for mine."

"Fine."

The pair followed the path of immaculate flowers that snaked up to the French door. Servers in tailored tuxedos strolled by while a pianist played in the background. She looked down at her jeans and T-shirt, and felt instantly out of place. She hated admitting Agnes could have been right about something.

After a greeting from a man with a bowtie, they were led to a booth massive enough to accommodate six people.

A server immediately approached them. "My name's Yvette and I'll be taking care of you. Would you like to start with a glass of Pinot Noir or an appetizer of Tomato Bruschetta?"

Ian looked at Dani. "You want an appetizer?"

"No. Just tea."

"Usually, people prefer that with dessert. Would you like an ice water to go with it?"

"Why's that?" she couldn't help but ask.

The waitress bit her lip as if Dani's ignorance was embarrassing herself. "Since tea is Italian, we serve it hot and unsweetened."

"Actually, tea's origin is Chinese. Dates back to Han Dynasty."

The only part of Yvette that moved was one flutter of her eyes.

"How about just that ice water?" Dani retreated.

Yvette happily turned her attention to Ian, who was covering his mouth to keep from laughing. He picked a beer on draft and the waitress eagerly fled.

"One of America's oldest brews," Dani said mostly to herself.

"You know a lot about drinks."

"No," she corrected. "Just useless information in general."

"Do you enjoy making people feel stupid?"

Applause erupted in the restaurant. An elderly couple in the distance announced their fiftieth wedding anniversary. Shortly after it died down, the waitress returned with a frosted mug of yeast-fermented malt, and water with probably spit in it.

"I'll have the veal marsala." Dani relinquished her menu.

"Lasagna for me."

"Alright." Yvette left again.

Ian spoke first. "So. What does someone like you do with their downtime? I'm thinking cloaks and daggers and telling kids Santa Claus doesn't exist."

"Spanish."

"Pardon?"

"I'm learning to speak Spanish. I want to learn all the languages. I already know sign."

"Really? Who do you know that's deaf?"

"So far, a woman I met at the clinic."

"Interesting." He nodded. "Can I ask you something?"

45

"Go ahead."

"Why did you break Travis's heart?"

She crunched on an ice cube and vaguely recollected the time Travis asked her out. "I'd hardly call refusing a party invitation is splicing his vital organ."

"But you don't like him?"

"Like him? He makes me repress vomit in the back of my throat."

He found that funny. "Can I ask why?"

"He's just like the rest. Pretends to care until he gets the girl in bed. Then sprints for the door like he's on fire."

His response was something predictable. "I take it you've been burned."

"Wrong. I don't date." She nipped it in the bud right away. "Spare me the *I'm equivalent to a freak* speech. Already heard it so much I could write a novel on the boredom."

"You don't date? But you're . . ." He closed his mouth, which made her wonder which adjective he was going to use to describe her. "If you don't date, how do you know what it's like?"

"I suffer from secondhand."

"A friend of yours?"

"What about you?" She changed the subject. "You don't have to bother lying to me."

"Why would I lie to you?"

"Because everyone is in a dick-measuring contest."

His mouth opened.

"Too crass for you?"

He still didn't speak.

"Moving on. Tell me something crazy you've done."

He seemed to cycle different stories in his head. "I've been arrested once."

"Once?"

"My motorcycle and leather jacket doesn't brand me a thug." He took a sip of beer. "If I tell you this story, you can't fall in love with me. But I guess that won't be a problem for you."

"Correct."

"A few years back when I was working at Dax Auto, I heard this yelping sound. I went around the shop. Saw this guy beating a puppy. I yelled for him to stop. He did, but only to tell me to shut up and mind my own business. I told him if he laid another hand on that dog, he would regret it."

"And he regretted it."

"I got charged with assault and possession of stolen property."

"Stolen property?"

"I may or may not stole the dog."

"What happened to him?"

"Oh, I still have him. He's a Siberian Husky."

Yvette came by to drop off their orders. After a few minutes of uninterrupted forkfuls, Dani decided to ask her last question of interest. "What do you know about Brent?"

His expression shifted to serious. "Why?"

She just shrugged. "He said nice things about you."

"Oh. Well. Brent's had it pretty rough. His mom passed when he was born. It made his dad hard on him, I guess. Got pushed into the military. Then after his dad died of cancer, he started working at the restaurant with his sister."

"Sister?"

"Liza."

"Woah. I didn't know they were related."

"Yeah, well, I'm not surprised. You know that expression oil and water? Liza and Brent."

6

"YEAH, WELL, YOU DON'T GET A VOTE UNLESS YOU WORK IN THOUSAND DEGREE WEATHER."

The man who masqueraded as a vigilante propelled off the building and soared through the air. He landed on the dumpster below without falter. His archenemy was caught off guard by his mastery of acrobatics, which ultimately ended with him crouched in a trap and forced to surrender to the man in the mask.

"Good heavens!" Dani's bedroom door burst open. "You think you could turn that down?"

Dani sighed and reached for the remote.

"Can't you watch this and wear those headphone thingys?" Agnes complained.

"You're blocking the TV."

"Hello?" Her grandmother waved her hand in front of the screen. "Are you listening to me?"

"No. I thought that was obvious."

Agnes sighed so hard it was like she released a decade of frustration.

"Shouldn't you be poking ear plugs in your ear right about now?"

"Can't find the dang things."

"Did you check under the bed?"

Agnes blinked, too stubborn to wipe the annoyed expression off her face. "How did your date go?"

"It wasn't a date."

"What do you call it?"

"A waste of time enforced by none other than my grandmother."

"There went that conversation."

"There went," Dani agreed.

"What are you doing up so late?"

"Haven't you heard? I go through my window at night and fight crime." She dramatically reached for her bottle of water. "I watch this to simmer down."

Agnes ignored her. "Have you gotten in touch with Graham Wright?"

"Who?"

"Graham Wright. My old attorney. He's been leaving you voicemails for a while."

"Oh yeah. No. Don't care."

"Dani."

"I figured it was some telemarketer scam wanting my blood type and social security number."

"Your father's estate—" Agnes's words caught. "Well, acres. They're in my name. I can't think of why he would contact you."

"I know why. Because it's nothing."

* * *

On the security monitors Dani watched kitchen staff do their mundane prep work. Out of boredom, she also read the hand washing and caution posters tacked to the bulletin board in Liza's office.

Usually, people came in here to get fired. Two people had since she started.

Liza finally showed up and made her way to the other side of the disheveled mess of a desk. "You're starting waitressing today."

Dani wasn't sure if that was better news.

Her boss slung a file cabinet open and issued a black apron and notepad. "Follow me."

They ended up in the infamous dining hall where servers rolled infinite silverware. When they walked in, everyone went quiet and stared at her. It was strange.

"She'll be training you today."

A girl stood up and introduced herself, but Dani missed her name because Ian winked at her from across the room.

Eventually everyone finished and Dani was all that remained. A few minutes into her solitary, Rebecca passed though. "Hey, girl."

She was caught off guard by the girl's friendliness. "What's up?"

Rebecca sat down. "Waitressing. Cool stuff."

"Yep, yep." She waited for the real reason Rebecca was bothering her.

"So, I heard you and Ian went out."

There it was.

"I'm assuming you heard what he did?"

Dani looked up.

Rebecca made a face. "Oh, maybe you didn't. It sucks being the one to tell you, but Ian told everyone you slept together. He was bragging about it in the kitchen earlier."

Dani's heart felt like it threw up.

"Ian is an asshole. You're not the first he's done this to." Rebecca retreated and left her alone in her misery.

That was why everyone was staring at her.

"How's everything going?" Her trainer returned to check on her.

"Tell me something. Did Ian start a rumor about me?"

The girl didn't have to say a word because her face answered for her.

"I need to do something real quick. Excuse me." Dani left the dining hall and went into the kitchen.

Ian was stirring sugar into tea urns when she found him. She shoved him and he collided into steel. "Stay away from me, you lying bastard!" She left without his response.

She was so stupid to go anywhere with him. Of course, Ian was an asshole. She had known this. For the rest of the shift, she avoided him like the bubonic plague. Her trainer was surprisingly nice to her about the whole thing, but her attempts to cheer her up didn't help.

When the restaurant closed, Dani found a stall in the restroom so she could put her feet up. It felt so good she could cry.

The door to the bathroom burst open and two girls walked in. One of them was Rebecca. "She went total psycho on him. Oh man, I couldn't have asked for a better reaction."

"You go, girl."

"Dumbass. She has no idea I spread it."

They both laughed.

Rebecca had spread the rumor. Why that didn't occur to Dani, she didn't know. She lowered her feet to the tile and opened the stall door. They hushed immediately and had priceless looks on their faces.

"Don't let me interrupt. Keep laughing." Dani walked out of the restroom and rounded the corner. The entire restaurant was silent, and everyone had stopped their side work and stared at her with violating eyes again. "What is it this time?"

Brent answered for the group. "Ian just made an ass out of himself."

"He what?"

"He made an announcement that nothing happened between you two. That you turned him down."

She closed her eyes. "Where is he?"

"Already left." Brent started toward the kitchen but stopped. "He's working at Dax Auto tomorrow morning though."

*   *   *

Describing Dax Auto as old and dirty would be a colossal understatement. It was difficult to find because the sign was faded and lost to the sun for quite some time. Only one garage was operational due to others being scattered with equipment. Unorganized shelves lined the walls with tools, coils, and foreign metals. The few workstations had become a lost cause with the piled-up tires and other unidentified mess heaped around them.

"Hello?" Her voice ricocheted off the metal construct.

She expected drums of gasoline to dominate the air, but oddly it was sawdust. The familiar smell of fresh cedar made her think she was five years old again roaming her treehouse. Her nose had not inhaled the scent since. It made her happy, angry, and sick all at the same time.

Something touched her leg and made her jump.

"Oh. Hello."

A beautiful white-and-black dog peered up at her with arctic-blue eyes. This had to be the dog Ian rescued. She kneeled down to pet him. He immediately rolled over on his back and let her rub his white belly.

"Good grief, Meeko. You'd take advantage of anyone around here."

"Brent?" She straightened. "What are you doing here?"

He was wiping his oily fingers on an even oilier rag. "I work here."

"Tell me something. Why does an auto shop smell like wood?"

He seemed surprised by her detection. "Ian sawed up some parts for a coffee table this morning."

"Speaking of."

"He's out back. Good luck."

She headed that way. What she found on the back of the property was a beautiful open field. In the distance was a cabin nestled among pine trees with a pond straddling its side.

A grunt came from her left. Ian's feet were extended out from underneath a truck, the sounds of a wrench tinkered in the wind.

She almost lost her nerve. "Ian?"

The wrench stopped for a few seconds but then started back again.

"I don't blame you for being pissed. I wanted to say I'm sorry."

He rolled out from under the truck and stood. Worn and torn blue jeans and a sweaty T-shirt hugged his taut frame. His skin had splotches of black grease and his hair was in dire need of a wash. He was gorgeous.

He held up his hand, the wrench nested between his fingers like a cigar. "You're apologizing? You're not about to burst into flames, are you?"

"I shouldn't have . . ." She couldn't think of the right word.

"Assaulted me?"

"Assaulted is a little harsh."

"Tell that to the dishwasher I dented."

"Look. I know I'm not the easiest person to deal with. But I'd rather be that than a pushover."

"Personally, I prefer neither."

"I despise how you're turning this into a joke."

"Yeah? If you despise me so much, why are you here?" He tossed his wrench in a cardboard box and made it flip on its side.

"I didn't want to leave things on a bad note."

"To be fair, we didn't start on a good one."

Her focus shifted to the tiny log cabin again. "Does someone live there?"

"Yeah. Me." He poured a bucket of black oil out in the grass.

"You know you're not supposed to do that, right?"

"What?"

"Poor that oil out."

"What are you, my mother?" He tossed the empty bucket aside. "Shit, it's hot." And with that, he pulled off his shirt and dropped it to the dirt.

Her eyes traced the curves of his muscle. She watched the sweat glisten off his skin. She looked away. "Oh my gosh."

"You got a problem?" he challenged her.

"I don't—know if you should—"

"Yeah, well, you don't get a vote unless you work in thousand degree weather."

She needed to leave. She stared at her feet and beseeched them to obey. "I need to be forgiven so I can go."

"Seems like you've got a problem then."

The sunlight illuminated a scar that traced his back. It reminded her of her own scar on her stomach. She almost asked him about it but didn't because that would mean she was looking at him. And she was not looking at him . . . "I guess I'll leave now."

"So soon? Got a hot date? Oh yeah, that's right. You don't date."

"You say that like it's weird."

"It is." He took a few steps toward her. She maintained solid eye contact. She didn't dare look down at his bare chest. "And just for the record, I wouldn't have told anyone even if we had slept together."

"Wow. Do girls actually believe that bullshit?"

"Excuse me?"

"I think you heard what I said."

He didn't bother defending himself. "You must know who started the rumor since you know I didn't do it."

"Does it matter?"

"Yeah. I think it does."

She didn't trust him to be mature enough to not avenge the situation. She had no loyalty to Rebecca, but attention is not something she wanted to give her.

"Let's just drop it." She backed away to leave. "Take my apology. Or don't."

7

"DINOSAUR URINE."

"So, how's life? Thought maybe you had died or something." Hazel was vise-gripping her hip, fueled with annoyance at being ignored the past few days.

Dani felt her teeth grind together. "Sorry, parole officer. Do you need a sample of my urine too?" She looked to her left and realized Ian had walked up unnoticed. "Hazel, Ian. Ian, Hazel."

Hazel's jaw dropped. "Oh my gosh. *You're* Ian?"

"I am."

She gave Dani a bewildered look and then extended her hand. "I'm Hazel Bloom. Her friend."

He shook her hand. "Ian Price. Still not sure if I'm her friend."

Dani ignored him. "What are you doing here, Hazel? I'm working."

Her friend seemed to struggle with refocusing her eyesight. "Birthday, your birthday is coming up."

She felt sick to her stomach. "So?"

"I want to have a party. Something small."

"Sounds fun." Ian leaned against the wall. "Are you getting a moon bounce?"

Dani and Hazel both looked at him.

Hazel touched her mouth to cover her smile. "You have to understand, Ian. Dani is so weird about her birthday."

"I am not. I just don't celebrate it."

"Like I said—weird." Hazel glanced at her phone. "Well, I have to run. Just wanted to stop by and make sure you weren't dead in a ditch somewhere." She turned to leave but got one last eyeful of Ian first. "You have to come to the party. And Dani, we're having a discussion later."

"Can't wait."

Behind Ian emerged Liza, her nostrils unusually flared. She pointed at both of them. "You two. My office."

This was going to be a wonderful way to start the day.

They followed Liza to her private chamber. She set the stage by slamming the door. "You mind telling me what this fighting is about?"

"Fighting?" Dani asked.

"Don't play with me. Rumor has it you two had an altercation in the kitchen."

Dani considered repeating the word altercation with a question mark, but it didn't go well for her the first go around.

"Who said we were fighting?" Ian acted coy.

"Oh sure, like I'm going to give you the whistleblower." Liza locked eyes with Dani. "Why did you push him?"

"I—"

"Are you two involved?" Liza interrupted.

"No," she answered sternly. "Not at all."

"Yeah, that would require her to be attracted to something other than herself."

Liza glared at him. "Is this a joke to you?"

He blinked. "That was serious."

"One of you better tell me what's going on right now."

One would think Liza was a prison warden of hardened criminals with the seriousness she was treating this situation.

Before Dani could answer, Ian did. "This was my fault."

They both looked at him now.

He shrugged innocently. "We were horsing around. There's this stupid game me and my friends play. Whoever is shoved last is the loser. It's really dumb."

"Dani?"

She kept her eyes on Liza. "Yeah. We were playing that dumb game."

"You two are coming in early Thursday morning to set up a reservation—9:00 a.m. You violate the rules of safety again, you'll both be fired."

Like working there was some big prize or something.

*　*　*

"You're going where again?"

Dani was perched on the foyer window seat watching the drizzle of rain and intertwine of grey clouds. The only sounds in the house were the ping of water against the glass and shuffling noises from the sewing room. "From how you forget things, I'd say you have Alzheimer's."

Agnes appeared in the doorway with a piece of green fabric clutched in her hand. "Oh honey, just because your boring life goes unnoticed around here doesn't mean I'm senile."

"Because sewing is intriguing."

"I don't view it as sewing. I view it as fashioning a weave to siphon the sun from blinding my eyes at sunrise."

"Fancy vernacular for stitching a curtain." Dani grabbed her stuff to leave, but something fell out of her bag and rolled across the hardwood. She turned around to see her grandmother bend down and pick it up. Even though she knew what it was, she squinted at the transparent orange prescription bottle. "Oh, would you look at that. Dinosaur urine."

Her grandmother's arm went limp. "You said you weren't using."

"It's not like it was."

"You know all drug addicts say that?" Her forehead wrinkled. "I think we should go back to a therapist. They can help you if you actually talk to them."

"How is someone who memorized psychology textbooks, who hasn't shared my life experiences supposed to help me?" She stood there and gave Agnes the opportunity to answer. When she couldn't, Dani left.

When she drove up to the restaurant, she noticed Ian's motorcycle parked close to the front door. She went upstairs to the big reservation room and heard grunt noises coming from the storeroom. Ian came out with a crate of wine glasses. "Coffee? For me?"

She looked at the two coffees in her hand and set one on the bar. "Not because I like you. Because I want you to work faster."

"You should make your own greeting cards." He walked over to the windows to open them.

"What are you doing?"

"Giving us some fresh air. Liza doesn't run the AC when we're closed."

"Of course, she doesn't. That would be too humane. What do I start with?"

"You can get the chairs from the storeroom. We need eighty."

"Chairs?"

"No. Pogo sticks," he answered sarcastically.

She mumbled curses under her breath and headed for the storage room.

"And hey, don't let that door close."

She came back out. "Why?"

"It locks from the outside."

"What genius designed that?" She went back in and started pulling at the banquet chairs. Untangling them from the cart they seemed to be superglued to was a pain in the ass. She struggled with the first three or so before she chucked one across the storeroom.

After she walked out, she put her hands on her hips. "Here's a thought. Instead of graciously setting out silverware like a jerk-off, why not help me in here?"

He laid down a stack of napkins. "Well. Since you asked nicely."

When she went back into the storeroom, she tried to yank another one out, but her back hit Ian's chest. She froze. She didn't realize he was standing right behind her. He leaned down over her shoulder and aligned his arms with hers. Her heart retreated to her throat.

"Do it like this." He slid the chair out with ease.

A creaking sound interrupted everything. They both looked in the direction of the noise.

"No!" He ran for the door.

It was too late. It shut.

They both stared at it before they panicked.

She swallowed. "Please tell me you have your phone."

He looked at her. "Mine's on the bar. Where's yours?"

She closed her eyes. "My car."

He ran his hands through his hair. "Well. That sucks."

"We can't be stuck in here!" Suddenly she felt like she was hyperventilating.

"Do you need a brown paper bag?"

"Shut up! There has to be a way out of here." She looked for a vent or anything that could get them out.

"There is. That door."

"You're not helping."

"And you are? You look like you're about to pass out."

"I can't be stuck in here with you." She pointed at him. "This is your fault. You did this on purpose!"

"Me? You're the one that called me in here."

"You're the idiot who opened the windows. I bet the wind made the door close."

"What about you throwing shit?"

"Ok!" She took in a breath. "How long are we stuck in here?"

"Probably an hour."

"Probably an hour?"

"Brent won't be here until 10:00."

She collapsed on a pile of boxes.

He slowly sunk down to the floor across from her.

She eyed him suspiciously. "You really don't have your phone?"

"You want to search me?"

She scanned his torn jeans and outline of muscle imprinted through his shirt. "I'd rather be shot with a dart gun than touch you."

"Why do you hate my guts?"

"What makes you think you're special? Maybe I hate everyone."

There was a brief quiet between them. He completely switched gears. "Have you lived in Riftin a long time?"

She scrunched her knees to her chest. "We're not doing that."

He looked side to side. "We're not doing what?"

"Bonding." She shook her head.

"If you have such a phobia for it, why did you have lunch with me?"

"Because my grandmother tricked me."

"You could have still bailed."

Her head straightened. "Oh, I see. I see what you're doing."

He had the tiniest smile tugging at one corner. It made pockets of anger in her rupture. "I know your plight," she began. "It's not an original idea by the way. I'm not one of your tick marks lacking self-respect that's going to sit on your stick."

It took him a moment to absorb everything she said. He displayed an array of emotions, and at the end found it funny.

"Did I say something amusing?"

He kept laughing. It made her more furious.

After he got it out of his system he finally spoke. "Do us both a favor and don't pretend like you know me."

"But I do. I know exactly who you are."

"Here we go." He threw his arms up in the air. "Need I remind you I fought off that asshole for you?"

"I could have handled it. I could have fought him off."

He snorted.

She angrily stood up. "Charge at me, you arrogant prick."

"Have you lost your mind?"

"Do it. Or are you a wuss?"

Everything went still.

He lunged forward and took her to the wall. She twisted under him and brought her arm up and clocked him in the face.

He took a step back, seeming to be in disbelief. "You just elbowed me in the face."

"Your point?"

He took her to the ground, straddled her hips, and pinned her arms above her head. For a moment, she was truly afraid.

"You do know self-defense. But I doubt you can get out of this."

She didn't exactly surrender. A deafening heartbeat in her ears was immobilizing her. She was very aware of his lower anatomy touching hers.

He leaned down, his respire touched her cheek. "Or do you not want to?"

"What? I—let me go!"

A clicking lock interrupted everything. The door to the storeroom opened and Brent walked in. He raised an eyebrow.

She harshly shoved Ian off. "It's not what you think."

Ian stood up. "Yeah, so don't ask."

"Wasn't gonna." Brent put a heavy box down to hold the door open, a brilliant idea Dani and Ian should have implemented earlier.

When they exited the storeroom, Liza was waiting for them on the other side. She was practically foaming at the mouth. Dani didn't bother defending herself, but Ian thought it was worthwhile for some reason. Brent retreated downstairs, eager to be away from the situation.

"Why am I not surprised? I have eighty people arriving in an hour and nothing's done." Liza only glared at Dani. "You've been nothing but trouble since you started."

"Are you kidding me?" Dani was past the point of fed up. "You know. You never apologized to me for almost getting me killed."

"It was an accident." Ian tried to intervene. "It wasn't Dani's fault."

Dani waved her hands. "Oh, don't bother. Who cares?" She happily gathered her things. "I quit."

8

"CAPTAIN SPACE GIRL."

Ian pulled up to the curb and shut off the motorcycle. "Wait here."

Travis looked distraught. "No way."

"Wait here or you're walking."

"Dickhead."

Ian walked up the pathway to the blue house with stark white columns. An elderly woman's pride of yellow flowers served as its perimeter. He tightened his grip on the box and knocked on the door.

A brunette answered.

"Hazel, right?"

"Yup."

"Is Dani here?"

"Nah. She's on a date."

He felt his teeth bite down on the inside of his mouth. "A date?"

"Yeah. She met this hottie in her literature class. He can recite poetry in French. Very beau beau."

When did all this happen?

He looked at Hazel and realized too many seconds had passed. He cleared his throat to rid an impossible knot. "Cool."

Hazel grinned. "Obviously you don't know her very well. This is Dani we're talking about. She's not on a freaking date."

He refrained from smiling.

"But it's good to know it bothers you." Hazel winked at him.

"Huh?"

"I'm not dumb, dude. I know you have a thing for her."

"A thing for who?" Dani appeared in the doorway. Her presence nearly precipitated his heart cardiac arrest.

Hazel causally cleared her throat, if there was such a thing. "Captain Space Girl. But then again, who doesn't?"

Dani rolled her eyes before she turned her attention to Ian. Some of her dirty blonde hair had fallen from being pulled back in a bun. She had no idea how gorgeous she was and wouldn't care if she did.

"Hey!" Travis yelled from the street.

Only Hazel gave him the time of day. "Hello . . . person." She waved back.

"I'm sorry you quit," Ian spoke.

Dani scrunched up her face with total disgust. "That makes one of us."

He looked down and remembered his reason for being there. He opened the black case in his arms. "I kind of got you something for your birthday."

"Oh," was all Dani muttered. There was no ounce of excitement in her voice.

"It's a .22 revolver. Nothing fancy."

His skin started to burn, but then she touched it. "Nice."

"I thought you might need it when we go to the firing range."

"We're going to a firing range?"

"I thought I could teach you how. To continue your self-defense training."

"I already know how to shoot. I've been to the range before."

"Oh." He was surprised.

She embraced the box, her grey eyes stared intently into his. "But thank you."

"How cute." Hazel was bursting to talk again. "I think I'm getting emotional over here." She fanned her eyes.

Dani was immediately annoyed. "Go die."

Hazel ignored her. "We're going to watch a movie if you and your . . . exiled bike friend out there are interested."

It didn't take long for Travis to run up the sidewalk and get winded by the short distance. "I heard something about a movie?"

* * *

The theatre was crowded due to the weekend. The four bought their movie stubs and sat on ripped vinyl booths in the lobby. Its patrons waited in anticipation for the doorman to arrive.

"I'm dying of thirst." Hazel headed for the concession stand.

Travis followed her lead.

Ian scooted closer to Dani. "Are you getting anything?"

She surveyed the stand before she answered. "No. I never understood why people have to gorge during a movie."

"Right."

She examined the cracks in the wall. The place really needed a fresh coat of paint but would never get one. She watched the dozens of teens stand in their cliques. They gossiped, texted, and acted superior like everyone else was a cockroach.

"Do you come here a lot?" he asked.

"No. Unless it's retro night."

"Now I have to ask why."

"The best films are old. People had morals back then." She watched the crowd part. "Ah, crap."

"What?"

"Hazel's ex is here."

Hazel returned with enough popcorn and drink for the apocalypse. Dani stood in a hurry to prevent the inevitable, but it was too late. Xavier noticed them. "Xavier's here."

"So the cheating sleaze is." Hazel grabbed Travis and kissed him.

Dani reached for Hazel's drink before she spilled it all over herself. She watched Xavier disappear into the bathroom. "He's gone."

Hazel released Travis and stuffed a fistful of popcorn in her mouth like nothing happened. "Thanks."

Travis readjusted his shirt. "No. Thank you."

They headed for the projection room. Hazel sat down first. Dani second. Travis third.

Ian stood over Travis and gave him a chance to correct his mistake. A few seconds later Travis surrendered and maneuvered to the other side of Hazel.

After the threats of making sure all cell phones were off, the room darkened and the film started. Dani adjusted herself in the seat to maximize her comfort. After a couple of minutes though, she realized she couldn't relax. The flashing imagery did nothing to tell her a story. She peeked at Hazel, who was stuffing her face and enjoying the movie. Travis was the same. It was just her. Something was distracting her.

Hazel leaned over and whispered, "Did you see that?"

No. No, she didn't.

"Something's wrong," Dani whispered back.

"I know. I think that guy is the killer."

"No. Something's wrong with me."

Hazel looked concerned at first. "You ok?"

"I can't focus."

Hazel's face shifted into a smirk. "It's a mystery."

"Seriously, what's wrong with me?"

"You want to make out with Ian."

Dani made a face. "You're never any help, you realize that?"

Hazel looked back at the screen with a smug look on her face.

Dani looked over at her distraction. He was paying attention to the screen like Hazel and Travis. She glanced at his arms, his face, his lips.

Kissing him.

The thought gave her a chill. It made her temple sweat.

Suddenly he touched her arm. Unexplainable shock waves tingled her nerve endings. "You ok? You seem fidgety?"

She couldn't tell him the truth. "It must be the chairs."

"Yes," Hazel hummed in her other ear. "The chairs."

"Shut up," Dani snapped at her.

Someone in the audience yelled for them to be quiet.

Ian lifted the arm rest that divided them and wrapped his arm around her. She counted the cost of embracing the rise and fall of his chest, the soap smell of his shirt. She straightened and peered at Hazel who was now intently watching her.

"I have to get the hell out of here." Dani left and walked herself home.

* * *

Ian rolled his bike into the auto shop and propped it on its stand. He reached for a wrench on a workstation and slung it with excessive force across the garage.

"Dartboard's in the office." Brent emerged from the back. "And we typically use darts."

Ian ignored him. He wasn't in the mood to joke around.

Brent reached down to pick up the projectile. "Where you been, buddy?"

"Nowhere."

"Nowhere, huh? Yeah, I've heard of it. Half-price beer at happy hour."

He relented. "I was with Dani."

"I'd say it went well."

Ian fished out a cigarette, lit it, and took in a nice long drag. "I think I hate her."

"Yeah. That's because you like her."

He sucked in more tobacco. The first hit didn't do it for him. "Have you ever met anyone like her?"

"Maybe in a past life."

"Me either."

"You want some advice?"

"Will it help?"

"Give up on her."

Ian took the cigarette from his mouth. "What?"

Brent went to the mini fridge and popped a beer can open. "You heard me. Give up. I've never seen you strike out with women. I see pretty young things sneaking up to your cabin at night. Don't think I haven't noticed."

"Are you going somewhere with this?"

Brent sighed. "Unfortunately. I was the same way, you know. Then I met her. Man. She . . . talk about difficult. She wasn't difficult, she was impossible. I did what was easy. I gave up."

Ian waited.

"You'll tell yourself she's not worth it. That someone else will take her place. But son, there ain't nothing that ever quenches that thirst again. Believe me."

Ian stared at his cigarette. "What happened to her?"

"Oh, you know. Ran off, married a good man. Married a man I could have been."

"The man you are now."

Brent came over and gripped Ian's shoulder. "And the man you can be now."

9

"INTOX—?"

The swimming area came into focus. Splashes of water erupted in the air while kids jumped in fully clothed. The other drunks had turned the area next to the pool into a dance floor.

Dani loathed Hazel's house. It was ridiculous in size and served absolutely no purpose. The lawn had hedges shaped into odd figures scattered among lime artificial sod. Expensive furniture staged every room inside, accompanied with overpriced art on the walls and so many scented candles it made her gag.

"Hey! It's the birthday girl!" Hazel ran to greet her.

Everyone clapped and cheered at the announcement.

"Who are these people?" Dani was already annoyed.

"Some I know. Others . . ." Hazel looked around. "I don't know."

"I thought this was going to be small."

"Would you have come otherwise?"

"No."

"There you go." Hazel took a big gulp from her cup. "Man, I'm glad they left town. Having a night to ourselves is much needed."

"It's sad your parents trust you." Dani spotted Ian in the distance popping a beer bottle open.

"He is so hot," Hazel tsked.

"Are you aware of the passed-out people in the grass?"

"Yeah, they got an early start."

It was somewhat alarming that Hazel was nonchalant about people on the brink of alcohol poisoning. "We should watch them to make sure they don't die."

"That right there—none of that. We're having fun for the first time in your life."

"I have fun."

"Sitting at home learning languages is not fun. Or normal. Tonight, you're doing what normal people do. Chug this." She handed Dani a cup of fizzing pink liquid.

"I'm not even legal to drink this."

"And if you don't, I'm going to punch you in the face."

* * *

"I really suck at this," Dani complained.

"You really do," Ian agreed. "You're holding the ball wrong."

"Is there a proper way to ball holding?"

"In beer pong, yes. Why are you gripping it like that?"

"Hey!" One of their opponents was growing impatient. "You going to throw it this year or what?"

She closed one eye as she sized up her distance. It didn't help she was a little buzzed. And by a little, she was a lot. She pitched it across the table, and it bounced and hit someone in the head.

Ian laughed because the person impacted was too drunk to notice. "I'd say you missed."

"I wouldn't say someone's head is a miss."

"Finally!" The impatient one got into position but slipped on something and fell. "Did someone piss on the floor?!"

His teammate shrugged and took a shot without him. He did a victory robot dance when he aced a cup. "So, how do you know Hazel?"

"How do you?" Dani countered.

"Physics."

"Hazel takes Physics?" Ian asked.

"I'm her lab partner, Jasper. She ever mention me?"

She took in the boy's appearance. Jasper's frame was petite and bony. The length of his sandy blonde hair was cut short, and on his nose rested a pair of red reading glasses. He was the polar opposite of every guy Hazel had ever dated. "Oh, you're Jasper," she lied.

"Sure am. Are you two close?"

"Cut to it, Jasper. What do you want?"

"Advice?" The boy nervously adjusted his glasses. "It sounds cheesy, but I was thinking about buying her tickets to the carnival next weekend. Would she like that?"

Dani looked outside the Palladian window and spotted Hazel next to the pool, making out with a guy. A guy that, no doubt, would be the subject of her next bitching session.

Jasper watched the pair kissing like his world shattered apart.

Ian poured him a shot and patted him on the back. "Don't worry, buddy. You'll get your chance."

* * *

After several beer pong matches, Ian crossed the pavement and took in the sight of the idiots in the pool. Some in their jeans, others in underwear, bathing suit be damned. He snagged a beer from a cooler and sat in a patio chair to rest his eyes. He had approximately three seconds of peace before Travis collapsed into a chair beside him. "Rebecca dumped me."

Ian opened one eye. "What happened?"

"You tell me, bro."

It took him a moment. "Wait. What's your problem?"

Travis stood with a growl. "Some friend you are. You don't even have the balls to admit it."

"Are you shitting me right now?"

"I'm so sick of women slobbering over you like you're something special."

Now Ian stood up. "Let's get something straight. I wouldn't touch Rebecca with a ten-foot pole." Out of the corner of his eye he noticed Dani across the way. She was busy talking to someone, her face frigid as usual. He could count on one hand how many times this girl smiled, and he had never seen her laugh. He wondered if there was anything in this world Dani Poe found funny.

Travis's eyes followed where Ian was staring. He kicked a chair. "That's another thing! You started things up with Dani when I liked her first!"

"What are you, five?"

"You can have her! A backstabber and a cunt go well together."

Ian punched him in the face. Travis fell back on the ground and cursed. Everyone close by stopped what they doing to watch.

Travis charged him and it took multiple guys to separate them. In the commotion, Hazel yanked Travis by the arm and threatened him to leave. He kicked everything in his path as he did.

Ian dusted himself off. "Thanks."

"That goes for you too."

"I'm not leaving. Dani—"

"Dani will be fine."

"At least hear me out. Travis is an asshole." He glanced around. Everyone had already forgotten about the fight and started where they left off. Just like the power of a TV remote, everything resumed to normal.

"What are you?"

Ian snapped his attention back to Hazel. "What?"

"So, Travis is an asshole. What are you?"

His mouth opened but nothing came out.

"If it's just another asshole thing for her, I will run you over with my car."

"Hazel, I punched Travis standing up for her."

"Fine. If you stay, don't punch anyone else."

* * *

Dani swayed in the dark. Her body throbbed with utter exhaustion. The simple lift of an eyelid took entirely too much effort. After downing shot after shot that tasted like window cleaner, she got a bit inebriated.

She realized Ian was carrying her to Hazel's guesthouse. She kept her eyes closed and listened to him struggle with the door while he held her at the same time. It was entertaining for some reason.

He laid her down on the couch and touched her cheek. "Dani, wake up."

She cracked both eyes open.

"I can't let you go to sleep. You're intoxicated."

"Intox—?" she battled to repeat the word.

"Drunk."

"I know what it means!" She sat up to prove him wrong but immediately laid back down when the whole room spun at breakneck speed.

"Try to stay awake. I don't want you to—well—die."

"I'm not dying." Though she wasn't entirely sure.

"You need to drink water."

She looked at him and put her hand on his face but almost slapped him because her motor skills were off. "You care?"

His eyes were stunning. Irritatingly so. Without understanding herself, she put her other hand on his neck and pulled his lips to hers.

He didn't pull away. He moved his lips sensationally over hers. She played with his hair. It felt like blades of glass between her fingers. He grunted and cupped her face and kissed her harder.

He suddenly stopped. "We can't. We can't do this."

He pulled away from her and sat on the couch at her feet. He started fishing cigarettes out his jeans.

Before he could light one, she leaned over and crawled to him. His eyes intently studied her as she did, perhaps wondering what in the world she was doing. Without thinking it through, her legs straddled each side of him.

"Dani—"

"Shut up." She leaned down and tasted his neck.

"Dani—" he said her name again but this time it was more of a moan. "You have to stop."

She touched him below instead. He let out a gasp, "Fuck."

His eyes rolled in the back of his head for a few seconds before he grabbed her hand and pulled it away from him.

"What? You don't like that?"

"Of course, I do, but—"

"I want it in me."

What the hell did she just say?

His eyes widened. His pupils were fully dilated, almost black. She leaned in to kiss him, but his hands gripped both of her shoulders. He lifted her off him and crossed the room, putting distance between them she didn't desire.

"You're drunk, Dani." He finally lit his cigarette.

"I am not!" she complained.

"Walk across the room to me in a straight line." Smoke expelled from his nose. "And I'm all yours."

"Walk across the room?" Her head spun at the difficulty. She noticed the cigarette. "Don't."

"Sorry?"

"Don't smoke."

"Don't drink."

"You smoke and drink."

"Your point?"

She frowned. "No point. Just wanted you to know you're disgusting."

He puffed his cigarette thoughtfully. "So now I'm disgusting?"

She watched his perfect mouth blow out smoke. The scene reminded her of a photograph of the "sexiest man alive" printed to make women drool. She rolled over in a fit. "Leave me alone. I'm going to sleep."

10

"THE PALPABLE INSULTS OR THE BURNING HATRED?"

The courtroom was eerily quiet. The only sound was the drumming of Kessler's fingers on the table.

Greer was sitting in the pew behind him and the state prosecutor. It had been a long, dreadful process but they finally had their suspect with a noose around his neck.

The sole survivor, the six-year-old girl, identified the tattoo on the killer's arm through photographs. He also purchased gasoline containers the day of the arson, and had no alibi for the night of the murders.

It was Greer's first major case, but he was certain it was an open-and-shut one. No way the court would not indict, and then a trial could begin.

He had been wrong.

The defense spun something about the validity of the child's identification of the tattoos. She had only nodded her head that it was the same and not spoken the word out loud. Why that mattered, he did not know.

Greer couldn't believe it when the gavel came down and the grand jury didn't issue an indictment. A trial was denied.

He was so angry, uncontrolled, and without discipline back then. The rage built from the interrogation, looking at the crime scene photos, and processing the extent of his appalling actions. He couldn't stop himself. He stood up emotional and pointed to the man with shackles around his ankles. "You sack of shit! I'll get you in prison! Just you wait!"

Kessler scolded him and the judge had him removed from the courtroom for mocking the judgment. Neither of those things could compare to what would happen to him after.

* * *

Dani rolled over and tumbled below. She blinked and painfully realized the hard surface she collided with was tile floor. The ferocious sunshine reflected off her pupils and emphasized head splitting sensations.

The light did that to her? She feared waking up to vampirism.

She looked around and recollected Ian carrying her to Hazel's guesthouse. She was in a room with a square television rested in the corner with two floral couches angled toward it. The place was packed to the ceiling with dust-covered sporting equipment. It was definitely Hazel's guesthouse.

Ian must have woken up and left because the couch where he'd slept was vacant.

Bits and pieces of memory folded into each other and secured no solid sequence of events. At some point, she engaged in multiple games of beer pong followed by Jasper drinking himself into a blackout.

She also recalled being robbed of a drink and carried to the guesthouse. And yes, she remembered kissing Ian, among other things—a lapse in judgment that would surely bite her in the ass later.

She opened the door to the outside world. The pool and courtyard were clean and pristine with no signs of a party ever taking place. Shoeless, she walked across the hot concrete and entered the side door of Hazel's house.

Her friend sat complacent at the granite kitchen island with a cup of coffee in her hand. "You get lucky last night?"

"Where are my shoes?"

"My maid washed them."

"Why?"

She shrugged. "Apparently you spilled something on them."

The smell of brewed coffee invaded Dani's nostrils. She went for the pot like a mindless drone.

"You need to drink water."

She ignored her and filled a cup with coffee and creamer.

"The dairy will make you sick," Hazel insisted.

Dani was committed to ignoring her and sat at the breakfast nook.

"Yeah, what would I know?" her friend jeered. "I've only been hungover a hundred times."

"I noticed the maid cleaned up outside."

"Cost me an extra two hundred bucks. Before she left, she yelled 'Pelotas!'"

"Balls," Dani translated and then pressed her fingertips over one eye as if it would magically cure her.

Hazel walked across the room to join her. Her loud footsteps made Dani want to strangle her. "You smiled a lot last night. It was weird."

"That must have been traumatizing for you."

Her friend twisted her mouth side to side. "So, what's the deal with you and Ian?"

"What do you mean?"

"You know."

"I don't."

Hazel sighed. "I guess I'll come out and say it. Are you two screwing?"

"Wow. Our generation has a demeaning way of putting it."

"You didn't answer my question."

"Gross. Why would you ask me that?"

"Because we're best friends."

"So?"

"We tell each other things."

"No. No, we don't."

"Why not?"

"For the same reason you don't tell me."

Hazel tapped the table with fake fingernails. She seemed to consider it rather than getting annoyed. "You can at least tell me if you like him."

"I don't."

"He's probably the most gorgeous guy I've ever seen."

"What has that got to do with anything?"

"Physical attraction."

"Then you date him."

"Why would I do that since you're in love with him?"

Dani lowered her cup. "Love? What crack pipe you been smoking?"

Hazel's slim contour of a chin fell in her palm. "Denial. Denial."

The lining of Dani's stomach bubbled.

Oh no.

She took off to the bathroom and barely made it before she hurled.

* * *

Dani woke up and realized she was boa-constricted in her sheets. She wiggled her legs violently to freedom.

A shuffling noise neared her window.

She went still.

When she heard the noise again, she retrieved the baseball bat from under her bed and made her way to the glass.

"Ian?!" She lifted the window.

He noticed the weapon in her hand and gave her a funny look before crawling in and landing with a thud.

She left to make sure Agnes hadn't woken up. Dani cracked her bedroom door to check. Her grandmother was lying perfectly still and snoring.

When she returned, Ian was relaxed on her bed like he owned the place. "What's with the library?"

"I get to ask the questions. What the hell are you doing here at one o'clock in the morning?"

Her harsh tone unmoved him. "You sound like an old man. Where's the suspenders?"

"Ideally wrapped around your neck as a strangling device."

She watched his eyes trace her body making her feel self-conscious about her thin shirt with no bra underneath. She crossed her arms to hide the outline of her breasts.

He leaped up from the bed and examined her bookshelf. "Is this some kind of self-help book?"

"No. It's about a psychopath."

"Because clearly that should have been my first guess." He picked up the thickest one. "Please tell me you haven't read this."

"Do I have to hit you with my bat?"

He ignored her. "I only read fitness magazines."

"That's not reading."

"Because it's not about fictional psychopaths?"

"No, because it's about muscle building like you need to be any more attractive." She closed her eyes and clamped her lips shut. "Hmm. I love the taste of foot in my mouth."

"Ah." He slowly placed the book back. "So, the truth comes out."

"I was referring to you as other females refer to you due to their shallow way of thinking."

"Right. Because you're above all that." He fingered through some of her college assignments. He picked up one of her textbooks and silently read the cover. "What are you going to school for?"

"Ian, do you think I'm stupid? Do you think I'm unaware of what you're doing? This is the part where you put on a charade and pretend to give a crap about my interests, right?"

He laid the papers back down on the desk. "Do you ever get tired of being wrong about everything?"

"Spoken like a true manwhore."

He took the role of serious for the first time. "God help anyone who ever tries to get to know you. And manwhore? Where did that come from?"

"Oh please. You're a walking checklist. I know you abuse it."

"When I was young and dumb."

"You're young and dumb now."

"What was I thinking? You don't need a relationship." He waved his hand over her collection of literature. "You got books with dust on them."

"Are you making fun of me?"

"Oh, I most certainly hope so."

She gritted her teeth. "I hate you with the burning fusion of the sun."

"So, what happened on your birthday was because you hate me with the burning fusion of the sun?"

She had been dreading when he would bring that up.

"Did you forget? That you wanted—"

"Oh, for fuck's sake don't say it!" She immediately realized how high her voice was and lowered it. "And that's not fair. It doesn't count. I was drunk."

"I've never done anything drunk I wouldn't do sober."

"Then you'd be the only one on planet Earth."

"Or the only one who would admit that."

She took a step back from him. His nearness was rattling her grip on sanity. "You need to go."

He walked toward her instead. "Something tells me you don't want me to."

"Because I've been so welcoming." Her feet took steps backward matching his pace. "Which part exactly? The palpable insults or the burning hatred?"

"Oh, Dani. You're so full of shit."

Her back hit the wall. He pressed himself against her, his arms propped up on each side of her face. The irises of his eyes illuminated in moonlight. In those eyes he could be forgiven every mistake, every aberration. It pissed her off.

"I think you fight bliss."

She glared at him. "And why do you think that?"

"Because you fight me."

His words jolted her. "How unbelievably arrogant of you."

His index finger raked across her lip. An act so simple felt like a current of electricity. "But true."

She shoved him off. "Ugh! I can't stand you!"

He smiled. "Go ahead and fight it." In one swift movement he escaped through the window. Before he disappeared, he retorted, "Good luck with that by the way."

11

"YOU WANT ME TO WEAR YOUR UNDERWEAR?"

Dani's peace while washing her car was short-lived due to Clare pulling in the driveway. Two other men climbed out of the pepper-red convertible behind her. Preston Tate introduced himself as the groom and Owen as the best man.

She deeply desired a mastered ability of evaporating into thin air.

Her cousin held up her hands. "I know you already told me your dress size, but I wanted to make sure since we were in the area."

After Dani tried on the uncomfortable dress that was the color of vomit, she came back downstairs. Watching paint dry would be more interesting than sitting with these people. She went with the excuse that she needed to clean up her mess outside.

The front door opened behind her, and Owen stepped off the porch. "Can I help?"

"With wrapping a garden hose? I think I'll manage."

"What do you say me and you hit the town tonight? You can show me the cool stops."

"No."

"No, you won't go with me, or no, you don't know the cool stops?"

"Both." She went back inside the house.

The conversation inside evolved into different types of high-heeled shoes.

Oh God, she had to get out of here.

She marched to her bedroom where her car keys were. After she searched her backpack and under every surface, she came back downstairs. She paused, turned, and looked. Her keys were hanging on the hooks in the kitchen. "Grandmother?"

Agnes came into the kitchen incredibly annoyed. "Could you be more rude?"

"I can, yeah. Did you put my keys here?"

Her grandmother glanced at the hooks on the wall. "Did you really just call me in here to ask me that?"

"Did you?"

"No." Agnes walked back into the living room.

Dani stood there and stared at the dangling metal. She never hung her keys there.

* * *

Black soot coated her lungs. The people in uniform spoke in medical terminology as unforgiving razor edges ripped her flesh.

"Ma'am, can you tell me your name?"

Reporters arrived on the scene in vans, satellite equipment strapped to the roofs like heartless emblems.

"She's lost a lot of blood."

Against their demands, she rose from the gurney in the ambulance.

"Miss!"

She watched her home collapse into rubble.

Her feet were cold and everywhere was dark. Ragged clothing flowed around her as she ran. Her bare feet raked the harshness of thorn and rock.

Smoke morphed into shadows that crisscrossed in sinister patterns. Their wings carried echoes of demented laughter and taunts of a foreign dialect she could never understand. Scarlet blood oozed from the crevices of the earth. They were infecting the innocence of nature.

They circled like vultures, revealing faces of rotted flesh, black eyes, and teeth sharp like sharks. Their ugly smiles burst into a fiery inferno.

Dani woke up with her heart thumping out of her chest.

It was just a dream. It was just that same terrible dream. She lay there and traced the ceiling, desperate to forget.

She felt the twitch, the saliva on her tongue. She knew it would calm her, put her to sleep.

She looked under the bed and opened the shoe box. The purposely saved birthday cards hid what was underneath. Her fingertips grazed the chalk texture. She stared at the tantalizing pills.

She had to get out of the house, or she would swallow them.

She didn't want to think about where she was going. She just grabbed her keys and skipped the thinking.

When she arrived, she parked on the street. The air was a little chilly, so she put her jacket hood up and navigated through the property, very aware of the fact she looked like a burglar. The dew from rain soaked through her shoes and socks. It was then she realized this was probably a terrible idea. He had visited her in the same manner, but it felt wrong when she did it.

She stepped up to the window. Ian was shirtless, sprawled out on the couch with Meeko asleep next to him. Headlights flashed in the distance, and she immediately ducked. A car started to come up the driveway.

She bolted and jumped over the porch railing but her jeans got hung and ripped in the chicken wire. She tugged on her pants. A car door shut, and footsteps neared so she had to stop.

Ian answered the door. "Rebecca?"

Dani felt her eyes expand. To come here was the stupidest thing she had ever done. She was probably going to be forced to lay there and listen to them have sex. She tried quietly tugging on her jeans, but it made a chalkboard scraping sound when the metal scraped against the wood.

"What was that?" Ian came outside on the porch for a second to listen but only cicadas answered him.

"So, me and Travis broke up," Rebecca said in a gross voice.

"And?"

"And, I thought we could have a little fun."

"I know you're the one that spread that rumor about Dani."

Rebecca went silent for a few seconds. "Ok? Can you be mad at a girl for being territorial?"

"I can, yeah."

She let out a sigh. "What's your problem? You don't like getting laid?"

"What can I say? My dick has standards."

Rebecca slapped him. "You are such a faggot!"

"Go home, Rebecca."

She stomped off the porch.

When she cranked up and left, Dani felt like she could breathe again and started tugging on her pant leg. She didn't realize Ian had come back outside for a smoke.

His shadow leaned over the railing. "Need some help?"

She froze. "I'm not stalking you."

"What?"

"I came by, and I just so happen to get stuck in your chicken wire."

He hopped over the balcony and tried to untangle her pants. "Yea, you're definitely stuck."

"Tell me something I don't know."

He used the flashlight on his phone to assess the situation. "You're caught in the wire underneath." He cleared his throat. "I'm going to say this in the least perverted way possible. You have to take off your pants."

"I'd rather die."

"Stay right there." He went back into his cabin to get something.

"Where am I going to go?"

When he came back out, he held out a pair of boxer shorts.

She squinted at them. "You want me to wear your underwear?"

"You can wear just yours if you prefer."

She snatched them and placed her fingers on her zipper. She stopped. "I don't need an audience."

He pivoted around on one foot.

She wiggled out of her jeans and slid on his boxers.

They awkwardly walked up the porch and into his house. She expected the scent of his domicile to be engine oil and cigarettes, but it was laundry detergent. He only had what he needed. A television,

93

couch, lamp, and coffee table. He lived in simplicity, the way she always wanted to.

In the light she realized she was covered in mud.

"You, uh, can use my shower." He pointed to where it was.

She headed that way.

After she stripped down and hopped in the shower, she noticed Ian's silhouette behind the curtain. Her heart leaped out of her chest.

"Found you some shorts." He put clothes and a towel on the sink and left.

After she showered and dressed in his T-shirt and shorts, she walked back into the living room to find him siting on the couch with a beer in his lap. "Want one?"

"Nope. I'll never drink again." She sat down on the couch with him. "So, what's the story of this place?"

"I just rent it. The owner of Dax is my landlord." He took a swig of beer. "I guess I should ask the obvious."

"Why am I here?" She didn't really have an answer to that.

"You look tired."

She yawned. "Yeah, but tired doesn't mean you can sleep."

"You have problems sleeping?"

"You could say that."

"How long?"

"Years."

"Years?"

"I—uh—used to be addicted to sleeping pills. And other things."

His eyes weren't judgmental. "And now?"

"And now I don't sleep."

He seemed to ponder hard about something. She wasn't sure what but didn't want a lecture. "I'm not a drug addict anymore if that's what you're thinking."

94

"That's not what I was thinking." He eyed the shorts he leant her. "I could help you sleep."

Her heart leaped out of her chest again. "What do you mean?"

He came closer. "You know what I mean."

Say the word stop.

Say the word stop.

Just say the word stop.

"Get your mind out of the gutter."

"What?" She blinked.

He pulled a blanket over her. "I was talking about reading to you."

"Oh." That made her smile.

He sat in the floor next to her. "Does it matter what I read?"

"No."

He began to read to her. Her eyes became heavy and somewhere along the way she drifted to sleep.

12

"YOU LOOK LIKE A SLUT FOR ONE THING."

People had described it as the white picket fence, the American dream. If any man had found it, it was Nathan Greer.

He had married a sweet girl with strawberry-blonde hair. After four years of renting a bungalow together, she found out she was pregnant. They did all the usual things. Doctor visits, reading baby books, and decorating a nursery. All that surreal gaiety was wrapped in him fiercely like unbreakable ribbons.

It had been a long day at work. Kessler was working him to the bone, pushing him to be better. He didn't resent it. He considered it necessary. After all, that's what mattered back then, excelling at a job.

The sun was setting with its colors of orange, and he had to call it a day. The smell of freshly mowed lawns and the innocent sounds of birds encompassed him as he shut his car door.

It didn't hit him like a shot to the face. It was subtle. It was slow.

He unlocked the front door and called out he was home.

No answer.

He didn't think anything of it. He just laid the mail on the counter after browsing through it and getting annoyed at the credit card offers.

He noticed his wife's keys and purse on the kitchen counter. "Honey?"

Maybe she was listening to music with headphones on, taking a bath, or went for a walk. The untruth to those things was like a map of possibility burning at its edges.

He remembered what it felt like when he opened the bedroom door and found his pregnant wife dead. It was like rusty needles pierced him asunder, leaving stains on his heart that would never wash off.

* * *

Ian needed a drink.

There was this nightclub called Skylit. The fact that it was two towns over was the basis of its appeal. No one knew him there.

He slid on the cold material of his leather jacket and cranked his motorcycle.

The club was always the same. The bar had reflective metal on the front that changed hues, reflecting the colors of disco lights. Its mecca was the dance floor and the DJ booth its crown.

He ordered a whiskey sour and turned 180 degrees on his barstool. This was the place of sleaziness. Its patrons were consumed in the elements of numbing the mind.

He blinked. He thought his eyes were playing tricks on him.

She was there in the madness of flashing light, her dirty blonde hair shifting with the colors.

He was certain he was imagining her. She was just an illusion, and he was losing his mind.

It was night and day. Her clothes were tighter. Her eyes had thick black lines of makeup around them. Heeled boots went up her legs.

A guy came over to her and whispered something in her ear. She nodded, and then he slipped a small packet into her hand. She opened it at her side and swallowed whatever was in it. Then she downed the rest of her drink.

She went for the dance floor. Ian watched the animation of her body move to the beat of the song. He couldn't take his eyes off her.

This was the girl he thought he knew, who never wore makeup, who only wore T-shirts and baggy jeans, who never did anything to her hair except pull it back in a ponytail. Now she was here, a completely different person, dressed in black, with her hair and makeup done, dancing around total strangers with drugs in her system.

My God, he felt drawn to her from across the room.

He patiently waited until she took a break and went for the bar before he approached her. "Dani?"

She jerked, her eyes bloodshot. "Ian?"

"Yup." He leaned against the counter. "To say I'm surprised to see you here would be the understatement of the century."

She turned her body away from him. "Hey, bartender dude, I need a shot."

"What you want a shot of, pretty thing?"

"Don't care. Just put it in front of me."

"I thought you were never drinking again?" Ian pointed out.

"I've been drinking a long time." She laid a fake ID on the bar. "It's just no one knows that."

"Not even Hazel?"

She downed her one-and-a-half ounces. "Oh, please. She probably thinks I'm a nun."

He leaned into her ear. "What did you take earlier?"

She shoved him away. "Get off me."

It hurt his feelings for some reason when she did that.

"What? Is it hard to accept I'm a drug-using alchy? Well, piss off with that. I don't want your preaching."

"Dani—"

"Another!" She shouted at the bartender.

"Dani?"

"What?!"

He placed his hand on her arm. She let him touch her for some reason. "I was just going to offer to look after you. You know, so you don't get raped and killed."

"Why do you have to look after me?"

"Well. You look like a slut for one thing."

For the first time she smiled. "I dress like this to blend in."

"It's working." He resisted the urge to trace his eyes over her again. "Why did you come here?"

She downed another shot. "My dealer works here now. Plus, I like to dance and tire myself out."

"Because you can't sleep?"

She nodded to the beat of the music.

"Dani?"

She didn't stop bobbing her head, her eyes were closed. "I'm not leaving," she finally said.

"Alright. You want me to dance with you?"

He figured that would ensue a hell no declaration or a slap to his face, but she grazed his arm down to his hand and pulled him onto the dance floor.

At one point she grinded against him, and damn, he didn't have the willpower to stop her. Her hair swept against his neck. It smelled so good. His hands found her hips and wanted nothing more than to rip those tight pants off her.

Something was happening to him. To see her broken like this, that she wasn't this perfect angel, it made him weak for her.

He turned her around. He didn't care if she was drunk, high, or out of her mind. He had to kiss her. She kissed him back, and it was the hottest make-out he'd ever had.

She batted her eyes. "Let's go to my room."

Fuck, that was hard to say no to.

She pulled him out of the hectic club and onto the street. Next door was a skyrise hotel.

"Why do you have a room here?"

"We're two towns over. I knew I'd be too messed up to drive."

"That's a good reason."

They went into the elevator. He inspected her in normal lighting. He could see every cute detail of her outfit.

They exited the elevator, and she swiped her key card.

"So . . . how often do you do this?"

She pulled him inside and shut the door. "What? You think I'm a whore now too?"

"That's not what I said."

She sat on the bed and unzipped her boots. "If you really want to know, I'll tell you."

"You don't have to."

"I'm a virgin. And no, I haven't had oral sex either."

"Oh."

She pulled him on top of her. She unbuttoned his jeans and her fingers traced the top of his boxers.

He wanted her. He wanted her bad.

He looked at the red in her eyes, her hair being slightly tangled, the smell of alcohol on her breath. If he did this, she would never speak to him again. "Umm . . . "

"What?"

He ran his hand through her hair. He had almost talked himself into it. "I can't. I feel like I'm taking advantage of you."

"Who cares. It's not like I have to save myself for anybody."

"It's still not right, Dani."

"When will you stop pretending?"

He titled his head.

"That you're this nice guy? We both know it's a lie."

He rolled off her and laid beside her. He propped his head up with his arm. "Why do you only want me when you're wasted?"

"I don't know. I hate you."

"Why do you hide this side to you?"

"Side? I like to get fucked up out of my mind. There's no side."

He waited.

She relented. "I put Agnes through the ringer. She put me through drug rehab, countless therapists, ER visits. I couldn't break her heart anymore."

"You're just cool with breaking your own."

"Correct! Ding, ding, ding!" She announced it like she was a game show host. It made him smile for some reason.

She turned toward him and mimicked his position. "I'm not always like this. Most of the time I do ok. But sometimes, I want to escape."

"Is that why you read so much?"

"Maybe. Probably. And if you tell anyone about this, I'll kill you."

He noticed a hair fall in her eye. He reached up and tucked it behind her ear. "Have I ever told you how beautiful you are?"

She shook her head no.

"You're beautiful, Dani. It kind of hurts to look at you."

(13)

"IT WAS WRITTEN BY A CRAZY CAT LADY AFTER ALL."

"I don't know what happened. I felt fine, then I was puking my guts out."

Dani eyed the dreadfully packed luggage waiting at the front door. The day had come for her to travel for Clare's wedding. "Agnes, I need to take you to a doctor."

"Don't want no doctor."

"Right. But I can't leave you like this."

"Don't fuss. You're a bridesmaid. You have to go."

"Clare would understand. And if she didn't, well, you know the rest of that sentence."

"It's her wedding, Dani."

"I'm well aware. My torture the last few weeks isn't imaginary."

"For once, can you please listen to me? If God wants me to die, I can't argue. Wouldn't want to anyway. You have to leave me."

The familiar sound of a motorcycle engine rumbled in the driveway. Dani went over to the bay window. "Ah crap. Why is Ian here?"

"He called last night."

This surprised her. "Why?"

"He was worried about you. Said he hadn't heard from you in a few days. Bless him, he was so sweet. Asked if there was anything he could do for me."

"Of course he did. And I don't like where this is going."

Her grandmother gripped her stomach, waiting for a pain to recede it seemed. "He offered to accompany you to the wedding and keep you safe. If I was too sick, which, clearly I am."

"Are you insane? I've been trying to avoid him."

"What for? Nevermind. I don't have the energy to argue with you." The doorbell dinged.

"Shit, Agnes!" Her foot stomped the hardwood.

"I love you too." Her grandmother rolled over to go back to sleep.

Dani went for the front door. Ian was on the other side sporting torn jeans, a leather jacket, and an irritating smile. "Hey, beautiful."

She shut the door behind her and fidgeted around in her pockets for her cell phone.

Hazel picked up on the first ring. "Bloom's pizzeria, extra toppings are ninety-nine cents."

"I need you to do something."

"Anything for you, love."

"Agnes is sick, and I don't want to leave her alone."

"I can stay with her. Question. Is your hot tub still running?"

"I hate you." Dani hung up and locked the house.

"You two have a weird relationship."

She turned and faced him. "Considering I found out eight seconds ago you were coming, I'm going to lay down some ground rules."

"It's always great to see you too."

"Saying I'm beautiful, among other things, will be off limits moving forward."

"I take it your panties are still in a twist."

"I—" She glared at him. "My panties?"

"You've ignored me ever since that night at the club."

She sighed. "Do you understand how much I hate myself for that?"

"Because it happened or because it happened with me?"

"A rhetorical question."

He touched his heart. "Ouch, that stings a little. It's not like I had sex with you." He got out a cigarette and lit it. "Which I could have by the way."

She grabbed the cigarette out of his mouth and threw it.

He stared at the cigarette on the ground and then back at her. "You going to pick that up?"

"And you were, weren't you?"

He held up a finger. "I thought about it. I didn't."

"You know, I don't pretend to understand what dumbass marble rolls around in your brain, but let me make something clear. It was a breach of boundaries that will not be happening a third time."

"Breach of boundaries," he mocked her.

"Yes. We are friends."

"Oh, darling. We've never been that."

She went past him and threw her stuff in the backseat of her car. Ian followed her lead and tossed his bag in the back with impressive force.

She glared at him. "I haven't even got the car cranked and you're already breaking shit."

"I didn't hear anything break."

She changed the gears to get on the main road. She noticed his vacant torso. "Seat belt."

"Pass." He stole a disc from the visor and music played through the speakers. "I would not picture you listening to classical music."

She slowed at a stop sign and leaned over to buckle his seat belt, their faces maybe an inch apart.

He smiled. "If you want to make out, let's pull over first."

She fastened the lock and leaned back away from him. He immediately unlatched it.

After about three hours or so, it felt like she got kicked in the stomach. The town of Grey Vein was exactly the same. Not a building, tree, or road sign was out of place. She considered it naive to think otherwise. Only in fairy tales did places crumble to dust.

After a large sign made of stone directed them down a road through the woods, she turned the GPS off. She started to see extravagant flowers, dogwood trees, and lit lanterns. The North Dalton Mansion resembled a castle. She had known about it when she was a kid, seen pictures of it, but never saw it in person. No element inside fell short of expensive.

A man wearing a red tuxedo greeted them behind a marble counter. After identification was shared, he handed her a room key. She turned and went for the elevator, wondering how Clare could afford a place like this.

They went to their room, and she laid her bag on a Victorian sofa. She took a moment to look around. The bed had a canopy, above were gold chandeliers, and the tapestry on the curtains were overly complicated with design.

Ian unzipped his luggage.

"If you think you're staying here with me, you've lost your mind."

He kept unpacking. "What do you think I'm going to do? Rape you?"

She swallowed.

"Look. It's one night. I'll sleep on the sofa."

"Whatever." She left him to meet up with Clare.

On her way down to the courtyard, a brown-haired boy in a pinstriped suit bumped into her. She recognized him from somewhere. "Do I know you?"

"A long time ago."

She racked her brain. "Farley?"

He grinned.

"I remember. We did an awful play about polka-dot flip-flops in school."

"Riveting, revolutionary," he joked.

"We have different taste in plays."

"Who can have high expectations? It was written by a crazy cat lady after all."

Dani had totally forgotten about her. Her mind drifted to her cat-themed classroom.

"How have you been?" he asked. "Are you doing ok?"

"Farley, I know you're trying to be nice, but please don't do that."

He cleared his throat. "I didn't mean anything by it. I'm just surprised to see you back is all."

She felt the overwhelming urge to walk away. "It was nice—"

"Bumping into me? We both know that's a lie."

They smiled at each other, and she went for the courtyard.

When the day came to an end, she was mentally and physically drained. Hazel had her tricks of torture, but Clare's spoiled existence and heedful attention to detail was a new level of eye twitching.

Ian popped out of their room. "You were gone a while."

"I'm sorry, dear. Let me get in here and run you a hot bath."

"That sounds nice." He closed the door behind them and locked it.

Them sharing a room together for a night was going to be a nightmare. She regretted letting him come. "I'm going to bed," she declared.

"With me, right?"

Her heart felt like it went into her throat.

"Joking. But before you do, there's somewhere I want to take you. There's this spot on the mountain that overlooks the entire city."

"I know of it. I used to trespass there all the time as a kid."

"Will you go with me?"

"No."

He cracked his knuckles. "You've got a long night ahead of you then. You're going to lay here, toss and turn. I'm going to feel bad you can't sleep. Except this time, I'm not going to be a nice guy."

"So, you are going to rape me."

He made a face. "Or you could come with me, we come back, you sleep here, I sleep in the car."

"You would sleep in the car?"

"Sure."

"What a charisma for talking people into things."

14

"HARSH, CRASS, GENERALLY UNPLEASANT."

When they reached the top of the mountain, Dani was surprised. It seemed higher and the town seemed farther away when she was a kid. Even still, the canvas before her was breathtaking. The thousands of sparkles from the lights of the town made the night sky different hues in color. She heard the faint noise of traffic horns and fading sirens. Even though it was a memorable setting, there was something eerie and not at all peaceful about it.

They were sitting on the back of the car when Ian interrupted the crickets. "I've been wanting to ask you something."

"Shoot."

"Why are you friends with Hazel?"

She was taken back by his question. "That's an odd thing to ask."

"You don't like her. You have nothing in common. Yet . . . " He didn't finish his sentence.

She didn't have to think about it. She'd known the answer since she was seven.

"Was she the only one nice to you at school?" he guessed.

She had never told anyone before. Not even Hazel. "Alright. I'll tell you."

He waited.

"In the second grade we were in the gymnasium doing these stupid laps with those square scooter things, I don't know what they're called. We did different positions and went up and down in lines. There was probably ten or so rows of us. We did one where you sat on the scooter and navigated backward. There was this overweight boy coming back and he didn't know his pants fell down and the top of his rear was showing. The whole gym echoed in laughter. He realized what was going on and stood up and shuffled to the back of the line, his face the color of tomato. I remember standing there in the nightmarish sound wondering why children found that funny. I looked at Hazel. Her face was rigid like mine."

Ian was quiet for a moment. "That's why you're friends with her? Because she didn't laugh at someone?"

"Hazel didn't think it was funny. She was the only one."

He played with a hole in his jeans. "Do you miss it here?"

"What? This dump?"

"You were born in this dump, weren't you?"

"Yeah, but how do you know that?"

"Agnes." He checked something on his phone and put it back in his jeans. "She took you to Riftin after your parents died?"

"How long did you two talk on the phone?"

"You don't have to tell me about it."

She considered the avenue but ultimately lifted her shirt and showed him her scar. "One of them stabbed me before they killed my parents. Burned my house to the ground. On my sixth birthday. There. I told you."

"That's why you don't celebrate your birthday."

"There were awful rumors at school. I stopped eating, became as thin as a skeleton. Then one day Agnes came home with cardboard boxes and said we were leaving. I was so happy I cried."

"What kind of rumors?"

"That I killed them."

"Your own parents? You were six."

She shrugged. She never understood it either.

"Why does bad shit happen to good people?"

"Show me a good person."

His whole body jerked. "What? Are you saying you're not a good person?"

"I'm saying no one is. We're human, we make mistakes. You haven't figured that out yet?"

"Do you—"

"Believe in God?" She craned her neck to look at him. "Yes."

"You don't doubt?"

She paused and thought about how to respond to that. "I don't doubt I ever made my heart pump a miraculous thing like blood. Or for my eyes to capture imagery. For me to take credit for existing would make me a liar."

He let out a long breath. "I don't think I've met anyone like you before."

"Like me how?"

"You're . . . too honest."

She thought about that. "Not everyone lies to you. I'm sure Brent doesn't."

"He lies to me every day. How he's doing, how the shop's doing. He wears shoes with holes in them and thinks I don't notice."

She wasn't sure where he was going with this. "Are you saying Brent's financially strapped?"

"He's worse than that."

"This is none of my business, but doesn't he have two jobs?"

"He doesn't get paid at the restaurant. He owes an old debt to Liza. Gambling, to be blunt. She works him to the bone and it leaves little time for the shop."

"How long have you known him?"

"I was thirteen when I begged him for a job. He let me sleep on a cot in the garage so I didn't have to go home anymore. So. Eleven years."

"Were your parents . . . "

"Abusing me?" His face answered yes before he looked away. "We should head back."

She jumped off the truck bed and slowly walked to the edge of the precipice. He didn't follow her. She felt holes burn in the back of her head. "Why?"

"Why what?"

Thunder cracked in the sky.

"Guys who chased after me always gave up. Very quickly once they realized what they were dealing with."

"What were they dealing with?"

She turned around. "Me. Harsh, crass, generally unpleasant. You've met me."

There was a long pause and it felt like his entire demeanor shifted into something else. "What makes you think it's complicated, Dani? I'm a guy. I wanted to have sex with you."

"Nice try, but I'm not buying. You can screw whatever you want, and there's better bits out there than me. Besides, I don't even think you have the balls."

He got off the truck bed and stalked toward her. "I don't have the balls because I refused to while you were trashed? Is that what you're saying?"

"You're dodging my question."

"Let me tell you something, babe. You point the finger at all the shit in this world, eager to criticize it when you haven't earned yourself a place on a pedestal."

"And what about you? You're some expert I need to take notes from? You look the way you do, and for what reason? So, every girl that's a stranger will suck you off?"

"Not . . . strangers."

"Not knowing whether or not you would marry them makes them a stranger."

"I never wanted to marry them."

She scoffed. "Right. You just wanted to invade the most intimate part of them."

Water started sprinkling. Neither of them cared.

"You say it like they're innocent, Dani. Like they didn't have a choice."

"Don't you understand what I'm saying? You don't give them a choice. You're a con artist."

"Oh, give me a break."

"You make it arduous."

His anger seemed to magnify inside him.

"Difficult," she translated.

"I know what it means! What makes you think you're above it all, not another cardboard cutout? You're a part-time drug addict. And you wanted me just like they did!"

Her head slowly shook back and forth. "That's the whole thing, isn't it? It boils you on the inside that I never wanted you sober. What a blow to that pathetic ego."

His jaw tightened. "Fuck you, Dani."

She went past him and climbed in the passenger side of the car. She threw her keys across the dash to make it clear she was refusing to drive.

He sat in the driver's seat but didn't crank up. They both sat there in the sound of rain pounding on the car metal.

"No more bullshit." His hand found his hair, water dripped down his face. "My life is a joke."

She inhaled a deep breath. "So is mine."

He looked at her. She looked at him. It was too intense for either of them to look away.

She straddled him and they kissed until they were struggling for air. She pulled off her wet shirt and unhooked her bra and let his eyes trace her nakedness.

He swallowed. "We can't do this."

"Why not?"

"I—I don't have a condom."

She kissed his ear and whispered, "I don't care."

He took her to the back seat and laid her down, raised her hands above her head and locked his fingers into hers. This was the first time she'd ever held hands with someone. His hands were callous and rough and incredible.

He kissed her down and undressed the rest of her. When he finished, he slid off his shirt and jeans. His voice was thick. "I don't want to hurt you."

"You won't."

He parted her legs.

"Fuck," he grunted. "Am I hurting you?"

Her lips touched his shoulder. "No."

The gentleness of his pace and the sheer focus of his eyes was the most erotic thing she had ever seen in her life. He put the tip of his thumb in his mouth and used it to touch her. His hips commenced, soft at first, then vehement.

There was no going back. Any sense of reason dissolved.

15

"PEACHES."

Dani blinked in the mirror, convinced a pencil shaving was lodged in her eye socket. At first glance she resembled a beauty pageant contestant and history would tell her that was not a good thing. There once was a period in history when pale, overweight women were deemed the most attractive. And tragically, most overdosed on hydroquinone to make their skin ivory white. Now it was tanning beds and a size zero, because someone, somewhere, said so.

The wedding promised a depressing harbor of lace and roses, corny wedding vows, and hokey harp music. The traditional candle-lighting ceremony was done, and a song played while the couple stared at each other while the audience watched awkwardly.

Weddings were weird.

She looked into the crowd and spotted Ian in a sharp black tuxedo. He stared off into nothing. His thoughts were his own. Her mind raced about the night before, image after image. Her skin felt hot thinking about it. It had to have been a dream. A man could not make a woman feel that way and it be real.

The bride and groom did something funny because the audience laughed and snapped her back to reality.

She squinted in agony. The heels under her feet had started to take their toll and the flowers in her hand made her nose itch. Photographs were taken until her mouth hurt from fake smiling and her eyes were damaged with a constant black dot in her cornea.

The ballroom reception was equally lavish. The dance floor was slick marble and so polished it looked like mirrors. Above was an insanely impressive mural, like Michelangelo himself painted it. Its edges had layers of intricate gold woodwork lined with red rubies.

She watched the herd of people at the extravagant buffet talk and laugh amongst each other. The only souls who danced were little girls, not yet shy from adulthood.

She noticed Ian drinking at the bar, so she joined him. "Hey."

He looked at her but didn't say anything.

"Are you ok?"

"Peaches."

"Are you drunk?"

"Trying to get that way."

"You want to tell me what's up your ass or do I have to play the guessing game?"

"Last night." He stared at his drink as if it held the rest of the answer.

"What about it?"

"How did the two of you meet?" One of the bridesmaids had walked up unnoticed.

"What?" Dani stalled.

"She wants to know how we met," Ian clarified in a decibel loud enough for the entire room to hear. "Should I tell her, sweetheart? Oh, screw it." He spun around on the bar stool. "You're going to love it."

Everyone in the vicinity seemed to crowd around him to listen. Dani braced herself.

"We started working at this restaurant together and she was so shy at first, poor thing. One day she was carrying out the smelly garbage to the dumpster and I was outside having a smoke. She slipped and fell on some rotten food, got a little in her hair." Ian peered at her with puppy dog eyes. "And I knew she was the one."

The group erupted with laughter.

One of the bridesmaids took a liking to him immediately. "Do you two have plans for dancing?"

"She doesn't. I do." Ian set his drink down. "Shall we?"

Dani slowly inched toward the buffet. Preston and Owen filed into the room in tuxedos. Preston whispered something in Clare's ear and the two love birds sat side by side and sunk into a universe where only they existed.

She turned her attention back to Ian with a burning sensation behind her eyes. Her heart thumped violently in her chest while she stuffed finger foods in her mouth.

"A pretty girl like you should be dancing."

She looked at a man possibly in his mid-forties, with tan skin, brown eyes, and slicked dark hair. "Sebastian Santos, right?"

"Nice ear."

"No, not really. The maid of honor is your stalker."

He seemed amused. "Hmm. And what about you?"

"What about me?"

"Why don't we start with your name?"

"Dani."

"Just Dani?"

"Just Dani."

She annoyed him into submission. "Would you like to dance with me, just Dani?"

121

"I don't dance." She walked over to a table and plopped down with a mountain of food.

Apparently, Santos thought it was worthwhile to follow her. "I can already tell this is going to be an interesting evening. With that look in your eye, I'd say you're involved with this fixation you're watching so closely."

Ian, he meant. "I don't know what you're talking about."

"Sure. No girl sits idly by while another girl gets her guy all hot and bothered."

Hot and bothered seemed like a stretch.

"What's it to you?" She took a huge bite of cake.

"A good way to spark a fire is by competition."

The idea of dancing with Santos destroyed a dear part of her insides. "Maybe you should find that maid of honor."

"Where's the fun in that?" He rolled up his sleeves and tucked the edges into the seam. On his forearm was a tattoo. It was two coiled snakes. She became mesmerized by its haunting familiarity.

He reached out to touch her, but she stood up to leave, convinced she was crazy.

He mumbled something that made her halt.

She turned around. She was almost deaf from her heartbeat.

"You speak Spanish, darling?" Santos rose from his chair, nothing short of amused.

Beads of sweat coated her temple and her knees almost buckled. "You don't remember me, do you?"

It was clear he didn't.

"Tell me. How do you forget stabbing a six-year-old?"

* * *

The nightmares were always the same. Violent shapes of empty color moving in ugly darkness. The floor being a vortex of liquid causing him to fall within. The killer's mad laughter replete with wicked intention chasing him down.

He would wake up tired to the bone, lying in a pool of his own sweat. He felt like he hadn't slept in a thousand years.

The only food serving as fuel for his maddening mind was black coffee and stale pastries. He couldn't remember what food even tasted like.

Greer had taken his time. He trailed Sebastian Santos, watched him, knew every little detail of the miscreant's calendar. Santos ran his illegal activities out of a sleazy hotel. It was a front for all kinds of drugs, sex, theft, and murder. He knew what was waiting for him on the inside: a bunch of junkies ready to erupt in senseless acts of violence.

The hotel was as inviting as a headache. Its tenants were cackling and howling like wild animals in a flash of flickering lights with the rumble of bass penetrating the peeling wallpaper.

He was here. Like a spider at the center of his web.

The person manning the front desk was surprisingly passing the time reading a newspaper. He was an older man with a thick, tangled, grey beard that dropped past his neck. His pathetic excuse for clothing suggested he was homeless. He spoke with missing teeth. "Nineteen dollar a night."

"Don't want a room. I want to speak to your boss, Santos."

"Ain't no Santos here."

Greer leaned over the counter. "What would it take, old man? I want to know where he is."

The man laid the newspaper down. "You some kinda cop?"

"Used to be."

"He kill me."

"I'll kill you. Might as well take my money and run while you can."

The man squinted at him as if he was weighing the truthfulness of his words. He wasn't a very loyal steward. "Three hundred."

Greer reached into his pocket and fanned out three hundred dollars.

"Five." He raised the price.

Greer held the stack up to eye level. "Four."

The old man reached out with black fingers to snatch it from him. "613."

Greer turned and went for the stairs, stepping over a drunk who passed out in an inconvenient spot.

He found room 613. He stared at the corroded metal of the numbers. He wasn't stupid. He knew better than to enter through the door. Once he knew where it was, he went back outside and went up the fire escape.

There was no glory in this. He knew that. He was no longer one of those heroes he dreamed about being.

He looked through the window and saw Santos sleeping on a sofa. The darkness of anger swarmed to him. He broke the latch and slowly lifted the panel.

He had been fantasizing about this for a long time. He drew his weapon and pulled a cloth from his coat to stifle his screams. Although in a place like this it probably wouldn't matter. "Wake up, shithead."

Santos's eyes widened and he cursed into the cloth.

Greer held the gun to his head. "I know you killed them. I'm going to take this cloth from your mouth and you're going to tell me why."

When he did, he was headbutted and knocked back. He was tackled before he could regain his equilibrium and his gun flew off in the dark. Greer was impaled by a knife Santos had on him.

And just like that, he had lost.

"You can't even kill a sleeping man." Santos gloated and stood over him. "Yeah, I killed your wife. I fucked her too."

Greer was coughing up blood and frantically reaching for his cell phone after his enemy left him to die. He somehow managed to call the police.

They arrived and stormed the edifice. There was no Sebastian Santos to be found. Greer wouldn't find him again. He forever vanished off the grid like a ghost.

16

"THAT'S GOD YOU'RE TALKING ABOUT."

Good grief, Dani's head was sore. She felt the harshness of light when she opened her eyes.

She realized her lips were sealed with multiple layers of duct tape while the rest of her was bound to a chair with the same unforgiving binding. It was so tight it felt like it was biting her ankles and wrists.

She blinked several times and recognized she was in a North Dalton hotel room, but not her own. She looked outside and noticed night had fallen. The last thing she remembered was leaving through the courtyard during the wedding when someone slammed her head against the wall.

And then, evil itself entered. His combat boots sent vibrations through the floor as if an earthquake followed behind him. "Superb. You're awake."

Santos took his precious time to sit in a chair across from her. His calculated dark eyes embellished him as the monster he truly was. Those seeing vessels were cold as ice sheets, absent of warmth, as if all decency had left him.

"What do you know? I got you in my suite after all." He spoke slowly like he was performing theatrics, which she preferred he'd spare her from. "You must be wondering why I haven't killed you."

Frankly, no. Her thoughts consisted only of sheer rage at this point.

"Can't have you tattling like a little bitch to the police again." Santos retrieved a shiny object from his pocket. He walked over to her and amorously rubbed the knife against her throat like a sick, twisted pervert.

She couldn't help herself. She rolled her eyes.

"Huh." To her surprise, he yanked the tape from her mouth. "Don't bother screaming. No one can hear you."

She spit out a chunk of her gums that had been torn when he slammed her jaw earlier. "What was the point of duct taping my mouth then?"

"I wanted to be the first to speak."

"Like a dictator. How original."

"I have a question for you."

She waited.

"You wouldn't know where he hid the money, would you? Does Agnes have it?"

She blinked. "What the fuck are you talking about?"

He looked disappointed. "Ah. Well. It was worth a shot."

"Are you going to kill me this century or what?"

He sat back down with a look like he was staring at weird fish at the aquarium. "Hot damn. Me and you could've had something."

She preferred it when he was playing the role of hardened villain and only trying to scare her.

"I guess that's a no." He said it like it was funny. "You aren't afraid to die, are you?"

"Sorry to disappoint you."

"You hate yourself or something?"

"Not the part of me that isn't me."

It looked like he was chewing the inside of his mouth.

Her head straightened. "So don't flatter yourself into thinking you're worthy of being feared. That's God you're talking about."

He stood up and slapped her across the face. It stung like carpet burn times a hundred, but she didn't let her face show the full severity of the pain. She straightened back in the chair. "You're not very smart," she said.

"I'm dying to hear why."

"If you want to kill me, why wouldn't you pick a better spot? After I'm found, they'll look at the security cameras and see you dragging me in here."

"This place doesn't have cameras, sweetheart. Anything else?" To her bafflement, he cut the tape that restrained her. He unlatched a gun from his belt and pressed the metal barrel into her scalp, tearing through at least three layers of flesh as he did it. She recognized the gun had a silencer on it. "Since you don't give a shit about dying, how about I remind you of someone who does? You wouldn't want me to slit Agnes's throat, would you?"

Her eyes found the floor. No, of course she didn't want that.

"This is how it's going to be. Poor traumatized Dani. Boohoo. Her parents died, and she can't take it anymore. She jumps from a balcony and kills herself. You made it ridiculously easy." Santos chuckled demonically. "Now write the suicide note. Don't give a shit what it says as long as it's convincing."

She thought about everyone she knew being told she'd committed suicide, an unsettling thing. Agnes would internalize it as her fault. "I'm not doing this. If you're going to kill me, just pull the trigger already."

He pressed the firearm to the point where it felt like it would crack her skull open. "Now, now. There are worse ways to die, wouldn't you agree? Your mommy and daddy didn't get that little luxury."

"You bastard."

"You don't want me to kill Ian too, do you? Your little dancing prince. His life cut short because you couldn't cooperate. I'd say you should write the letter."

She knew it didn't matter either way. No contract would be honored by him. He would kill them just because he felt like it.

She stared at the writing utensil, a nice sharp object he had placed in her hands. She had seen this nail-biter scene in movies. It was a tired old scene. The victim was always smart enough to get away. Turns out, she wasn't as smart as them.

There was a ringing in her ears.

It was a beeping of some kind.

A cell phone.

He pulled the gun away from her cranium and answered it. "Kind of busy here."

She considered stabbing him in the neck with the pen, but instantly laid that idea to rest. As soon as she charged him, he would shoot her.

Santos walked around a little. "Where am I? What's it to you?"

There was a voice yelling at him on the other end, possibly a woman. The idea of this man having a romantic relationship bewildered her.

She eyed the balcony door.

Santos lowered the phone. "I'm taking a piss. Be done by the time I get back. And don't get cocky. There's nowhere to go." He went into the bathroom but left the door open.

This was her only chance. His arrogance was the only thing she had to work with.

She tiptoed to the balcony door and surveyed the distance below. No way she could survive the fall. That was the point.

Come on, think.

She couldn't run by the bathroom and go out the door.

She only had one option. Go out and lower herself to the balcony below. If she stayed, she died. This way she had a microscopic chance of surviving.

She took a deep breath because she knew once she opened the sliding glass door, the noise would send him running back in.

She jerked the door open and lowered herself to where she gripped the bottom of the railing. She doubted she could successfully grab the balcony frame below, but shit, she had to try.

Before she could let go, Santos pulled her back up and shoved her inside. He kicked her ribs until she tasted copper in her mouth.

"You little bitch. I tried to be reasonable, but that's over and done with. I'm really going to enjoy beating the shit out of you." Santos went to grab her feet, but she twisted her foot and kicked him in the face. She crawled away and got to her feet.

He grabbed her by the arm and yanked it so hard it felt like it came out of socket. He slammed her up against the wall and choked her. She didn't think the depth his fingers were reaching was physically possible without snapping her windpipe.

She waited for the right moment and kneed him. He stumbled back, and by the grace of God, his gun fell from his pants.

She went for it, as did he, so she used all her adrenaline to kick him as hard as she could in the face. He cried out and stumbled back again.

She grabbed the gun and cocked it to ensure a bullet was in the chamber and aligned the square notch sight on his torso. She feared inaccuracy due to her nerves if she aimed at his head, a smaller target.

He squinted at her, holding his face. "I underestimated you."

"It would appear that way."

He smiled. The curve portrayed nothing but nervousness. His once certitude had been so easily demolished with the tip in her favor.

She remembered the cold basement floor cradling her spine. She was certain it wasn't real then. It was only a dream. Things like that only happened in movies, books, dreams. She would wake up because it wouldn't be real.

It was cold.

Her stomach was so cold.

Sticky red covered her petite hands.

He opened the basement door and spoke in Spanish. "Me hare cargo de ello."

She saw the tattoo of the two serpents on his arm before he shoved her down the basement stairs. The fall felt like eternity. It bruised her body and shattered her kneecap. When she collided with the concrete, he slammed the door and abandoned her to dark oblivion.

The slit in her abdomen couldn't compete with the horrendous sounds above her. She could hear her mother and father's screams. She had never heard screams like that. She would never forget screams like that.

She reached out for something, anything. Nothing but air greeted her grasp.

The grey smoke slithered above her when the house was lit on fire. The suited firefighters would shatter the basement window and rescue her, unable to do the same for her parents.

"You're no killer." Santos snapped her back to the here and now. "Maybe you're smarter than your father. Maybe the reason why you haven't killed me is because you know what I'm worth."

She might have laughed if she could remember how.

"I could set you up for a lifetime. More money than you could dream of."

It was a tough pill to swallow. The man who slaughtered her family was trying to bargain with her. "I don't dream about cotton and linen. I dream about listening to my mother and father die and I can't do a damn thing about it."

There was no ounce of emotion on his face.

"Do you remember stabbing me?" She gripped her aim. It did not feel empowering to be pointing a gun at a human being. She hated it.

"You want me to say I'm sorry? That I feel bad about it? You want me on my hands and knees begging before you splatter my brains on the wall?"

What she wanted. What a concept. The innocence of childhood? The silliness of laughter? She would settle for simply sleeping again.

"I don't want to kill you. I want you to pick up that cell phone and turn yourself in."

He lowered his hands, but not to reach for his phone. "Oh, honey. You've made a terrible mistake."

Her finger flirted with the trigger.

"You never admit you won't shoot them."

There was complete stillness in the room before he lunged at her. She fired the gun.

She watched him cry in agony and writhe on the floor until he went still.

She closed her eyes. "I said I didn't want to. I didn't say I wouldn't."

17

"OUR ASSES WILL BE SIPPING MARTINIS IN ITALY OR WHEREVER THE SHIT."

"Grandmother, I'm safe, stop screaming!"

Agnes was frantic, which was fair, but still deafening to an eardrum.

Dani informed the front desk, the cops were called, and now she was waiting in the lobby for them to arrive. She gripped her ribs. When her adrenaline rush dissipated, the kicks prior settled in sharp sensations.

"Ian called. He was looking for you," Agnes fretted.

"I already texted him where I was. He's on his way."

A loud crack interrupted them. She lowered the phone and went around the corner. It looked like the clerk had been hit over the head with something and was out cold.

Oh my God.

She sprinted for the exit and ran down the road leading to the mansion. She could hear someone following her so she veered off to the left hoping to lose them through the woods, at least until the police could get there. She kept running through the darkness. She didn't know what was happening but running seemed to make sense.

Out of nowhere she helplessly collapsed into a hole and her phone went flying off into the black. Thankfully she hit just right, and it didn't wreck her ankle. She was going to get her leg out and keep running but she heard footsteps too close for comfort. She remained still and hoped they would pass her.

Her pursuer walked with caution, leaves crunching under their heels. She held her breath as they passed.

They furthered their distance until she couldn't hear them anymore, unless they had stopped walking altogether. The possibility terrified her, but if she didn't abandon this hole she would eventually be found anyway. She tried to remain as quiet as possible as she pulled herself out.

There were more footsteps behind her. It suddenly occurred to her there was more than one person looking for her.

Something clocked her in the face and she fell into the dirt.

A face floated between the trees and came into the moonlight. "There you are."

The silhouette and the three indistinct shadows behind came closer. It was straight out of a nightmare. Dani's.

"Clare?"

"Oh, Dani," her cousin tsked. "It's not in your nature to not be difficult, is it?"

Dani was rendered speechless.

"I'm going to cut to the chase. We want your money."

"Well. You're robbing the wrong person."

"Yeah, I don't think so." Clare pulled out a brown envelope from her jacket. "The funds got transferred into your account four days ago."

"What funds?"

"They were thieves. Santos, my dad, yours. The last job they pulled was a jewelry store. Biggest score they ever did. Problem is your dad bailed and took the eight million for himself after the diamonds were sold."

She was positive her cousin had lost her mind.

"Santos and my dad were in your house that night to get the money back. But it wasn't there. You know why? Because your dad thought he was clever by hiding it in your name. And since the beneficiary couldn't touch it until their twentieth birthday, that makes you a millionaire."

"No, no way. Agnes would have told me."

"Only if she knew about it. The name Graham Wright ring a bell?"

She remembered a lawyer from Grey Vein trying to get a hold of her. Something about funds being transferred to her old credit union account. At the time, she thought it was bullshit. "Ok. Let's say I believe you. If you need me alive, why did you send Santos to kill me?"

"I'm not responsible for that dickhead. Santos didn't know anything about it. My dad is the one who figured it out. Made the mistake of boasting about it in earshot of his daughter."

"Why not just show up in Riftin and rob me instead of dragging me here to a wedding?"

"To get you alone for one." Clare straightened her gun arm and walked toward her. "I knew a wedding for the last shred of your family would be the only thing that would get you here."

Turns out, it wasn't. "I'm guessing you want the money to take back to your dad?"

Her cousin laughed. "I doubt it would do him any good considering Preston shot him in the head. Or at least, the police will think you did."

Dani's stomach twisted in more knots. "What do you mean?"

Clare had a sick smile spread across her face. "Well. I guess it doesn't have to be a secret anymore."

"What doesn't?"

One of the three figures shifted in the dark and removed their hood.

Her heart sank.

She saw the shine of his beautiful eyes and spiked black hair.

"Ian is one of us, darling. Has been this *whole* time."

Dani couldn't stop the screaming in her head. All the madness flooded in, the puzzle pieces came together. She took a step back, held on to a tree to steady herself. She felt like puking.

"The gun Ian gave you is the same gun used to kill my dad. And while you and Ian were sightseeing last night, we planted his blood in your hotel room, the revolver, even an apology letter from him. And let's just say Agnes wasn't too sick to travel by the stars aligning."

"What did you do to her?"

"What did Ian do to her? He stole your house key and took care of it while you were sleeping."

Owen and Preston took a step forward, but Dani boldly stepped back. "You can have all the money, Clare. But you're not framing me for murder."

"Well, someone's got to take the fall for it. And what makes you think you're calling the shots?"

"You know I'm not a liar, Clare. You know I would have given you the money."

"I do know. I know you would never let it go. I know where your moral compass points. We're the bad guys. Bad guys who manipulated you like a little puppet."

Owen interrupted them. "Are we done jerking each other off? We need to get out of here."

Clare ignored him. "You killed Santos, Dani. Or did you forget that already?"

"He didn't give me a choice."

"And neither are we." Owen pulled Dani's arms behind her back and tied them with her face crammed in the dirt.

* * *

The place was crowded due to the weekend. It smelled like cigarettes, vomit, and urine. Ian snagged his usual seat at the bar. "Whiskey sour."

"I need your ID."

"You're kidding me. I come in here all the time."

"ID."

Ian reached in his pocket and slammed it on the counter.

It wasn't long before the girl eyeing him across the way came over. "Hi, handsome."

He didn't bother looking. He was too tired to care.

"How about you buy me a drink?"

The bartender set down his liquid courage and Ian downed it instantly. "Why? So, you'll go home with me to tonight?"

"You say that to all the girls?" She sat next to him and slid her hand down his leg.

He looked out the window and saw her. She was smoking a cigarette outside. "Shit."

139

"What's wrong, pretty eyes?"

He laid a twenty on the bar and walked outside.

Her fake blonde hair was damp from the rain. "I got a job for you," she said with no ounce of innocence in her voice.

"How did you find me?"

"Where else do you go? Always drowning your feelings with liquor like a pussy."

"I told you to stay away from me."

Clare inhaled her tobacco. "Yeah. Figured you might say that again." She extended him a cigarette.

He refused it.

Being friends with Preston had put him in a lot of bad situations. One thing led to another and eventually Ian was beating up people he didn't know or for what reason. He only knew that he was getting paid to do it. It came with the territory from hanging out with the wrong crowd too long.

"I figured I couldn't sweet talk you with just a little money this time. How about a lot?"

"I'm done, and not just with you."

"Ah, shucks. Preston no longer your BFF?" She said it with smug satisfaction in her voice.

He started to walk away.

"How about a third of eight million?"

He stopped.

"Yeah . . . figured that might get those pretty legs to stop walking." She stalked toward him. Smoke expelled from her nose like a dragon. "I know about your little stepdaddy issue. Sounds like it's just what Brent needs to get away from that Liza bitch."

He regretted ever telling Preston about that.

The only sound between them was the buzzing of a streetlight and the sprinkle of rain.

She leaned against the brick. "If you're thinking of taking the high road, I'll tell you, I can make your life a living hell."

"Close enough."

"You do this job for me, you won't have to worry about us causing trouble anymore. Our asses will be sipping Martinis in Italy or wherever the shit."

"I thought I was already rid of you. Preston moved to Grey Vein to join your little mob you got going on."

"Mob?" she snorted. "Eh. Well. Might as well call it that."

He cracked his knuckles. "I do this for you, we're done for good."

She grinned. "Alright, handsome. I got this cousin."

"So?"

"So, I need someone to keep an eye on her. Be her boyfriend, that kind of thing."

He rolled his eyes. "Oh geez. Get someone else for that bullshit."

"Oh, don't play the modest game. I need you for the same reason I fantasize about you. If Dani is anything, it's not easy. And it'd certainly help to use the most gorgeous guy I've ever laid eyes on."

* * *

Fuck.

Clare had spoken it into existence. Her cousin would be difficult. At the time, Ian didn't believe her.

He noticed the boxes of paper towels in Liza's van earlier. He betted on her getting the cashier to do the grunt work of bringing them in. He knew the only duty Liza stood in for was taking people's money. Everything else was beneath her.

"I need a smoke break. Watch my tables," he ordered Travis before stepping out the back.

He knew he would be out there. With it an hour of closing time, he would be waiting for the kitchen staff to throw away leftover food in the dumpster.

"Hey, Vinny."

The homeless man looked up. He smelled particularly putrid tonight.

He wondered how much it would cost him to scare Dani in the parking lot. Turns out it was two hundred. He just left out the part where Vinny would get arrested and have the crap kicked out of him.

18

"I BET YOUR REALTOR LAUGHED
ALL THE WAY TO THE BANK."

Dani was left alone with Clare and Preston while Owen and Ian got the cars. The only ones speaking now were the thousand crickets. There was an aching in every inch of her existence. She sat there on the terra firma demoralized and defeated.

Eventually the sound of two cars came down a hidden path in the woods. Owen shoved her in the back seat of one. He claimed the driver's side and followed another car that no doubt had Ian, Clare, and Preston in it.

"Bet you wish you'd been nicer to me," Owen taunted.

She noticed his twitchy movements. It was clear he was on some type of drug. "I take back nothing I said to you."

She watched the shapes of blackness pass the window. It made her feel more helpless the further they inched into unfamiliar territory. "You're driving two cars?"

He eyed her through the rearview mirror. "Yeah, so?"

"Clare and Preston's idea?"

"What are you getting at?"

She shrugged. "Easier to frame your death that way. Drive your car into the river with you in it. Especially with drugs in your system."

"Shut up!"

"Gives them privacy on the drive there to plan without you around. Eight million sounds better split fewer ways."

"I told you to shut your mouth!"

"If Clare would have her own father killed, what makes you think she'd have reservations about your worthless ass?"

"You stupid bitch. I know what you're doing. Don't you say another damn word!"

She caught his worried flush in the mirror. It made her smile on the inside.

When they arrived, Owen yanked her out of the car.

"I bet your realtor laughed all the way to the bank. This place is a hole."

Owen shoved Dani to the ground and kicked her. "What did I tell you, bitch?"

"Don't fucking touch her." Ian shoved Owen.

She laid on the cold earth and coughed. The pain in her ribs flared up again. Ian tried to help her up, but she slapped his hand away. "Don't touch me!"

"What a turn," Owen jeered. "Just last night you were letting him pump between your legs."

Ian gripped him by the shirt. "Shut the fuck up."

"Guys," Preston intervened. "Stop it or I'll shoot you both."

Ian seemed to be considering his options. He released Owen, who fell back in line with Clare and Preston.

Something was happening. Dani could see it. It was an invisible line that divided them.

It wasn't lost on Ian what they were thinking. "What?!"

Preston said it. "Whose side are you on?"

"Oh, fuck off with that." Ian came over and pulled Dani to her feet. "I've never been on any of your sides. I just want my money."

Dani was led inside a drafty warehouse. There was something overwhelming about the air that made her skin itch. For the second time of the night, she was tied to a chair in the middle of a room. The four went for the exit as a unit.

"We'll see you Monday," Preston clarified.

They were talking to Ian because he protested. "What? I'm not watching her. That's your job."

"No way. Me and Clare got better shit to do and Owen's high as a kite right now. With how pissed he is, he's likely to shoot Dani in the face."

"For sure," Clare agreed flatly.

"You just gotta get through tonight and Sunday. Piece of cake." Preston slid the metal door down.

Ian stood there for a solid minute or so. Dani watched him clench his fists over and over. When he turned around, she immediately looked away.

He slowly walked toward a ragged couch across from her. He sat down, pulled a pistol from his pants, and laid it next to him. He actively stared at the floor so he wouldn't have to look at her. It made her furious he was too much of a coward to.

"I guess I know why you were chasing after me. Glad that's cleared up."

Of course, he expected this. It was definitely the reason he didn't want to get stuck watching her. "Don't start, Dani."

"Right. Like I'm going to cater to you now."

"I'm doing this for Brent. You don't understand what Liza is."

"I think I have a pretty good idea."

"It's worse. I'm getting Brent away from her."

She remembered Brent's old gambling debt. "That's how you justify it? Every time you look at him, you're going to think about what you did."

He rubbed his eyes. He seemed more annoyed than troubled with the idea.

"I wished I had listened to my instinct and stayed away from you."

"We're not going to hurt you."

"No? You're going to frame me for my uncle's death, stick me in prison for God knows how long while you ride off in the sunset with a sack full of worthless money. Am I missing something?"

He didn't flinch. Her words portraying him as a bad guy wasn't doing anything to him.

"That's why you were mad about the rumor Rebecca spread. You didn't care about me. Screw me. It derailed your credibility."

He didn't deny it.

"And that night you snuck through my window. To what? Steal my keys? You're the one that hung them up in the kitchen. How did you even poison Agnes?"

"She'll be fine."

"That's not an answer!"

He took in a deep breath. "I put a pill in her medicine case."

The act was so wrong it was hard for her mind to wrap around it. "What kind of pill?" Though she was almost too scared to know.

"You don't need to worry about it."

"Well, I am worried about it! That is my grandmother, you asshole!"

"Dani, she'll be ok."

"Oh my God." Something else hit her. "Did you get that guy in the parking lot to harass me?"

"I told him to scare you. Not hit you."

"You're the one that got me that job. This whole time I thought it was Clare." To think about the lengths he went to was unsettling. "You are such a liar. You did all that just to isolate me. Do you know how sick that is?"

It seemed like he had been pumping himself up for this moment. It would take a lot to crack his armor, if not impossible.

"If Brent knew what you were doing, he would turn you in."

"What makes you think you know him?"

"I know him."

He looked at her. "Like you know me? The liar who took your virginity last night?"

His words cut her, humiliated her, stripped her of any dignity she had left.

He dug a lighter out of his pocket.

"Why did you have sex with me?"

Her words interrupted him from lighting a cigarette. For the first time, it looked like he felt a remnant of shame.

"Come on. Nothing to lose anymore. Was it because you could or because you needed to get off?"

"I never wanted that to happen." He rubbed his eyes again. "I am sorry about that."

"Which part? Ruining my life or sticking your dick in me?"

He angrily stood up. "What do you want from me?"

"You're kidding, right? I'm in a warehouse tied to a fucking chair."

"I mean, what do you want me to say? It doesn't matter what I say anymore."

"Be straight with me. Give me that."

"You straddled me, Dani. Stuck your tits in my face."

"Bullshit! That's not the reason and you know it's not!"

"Fine!" He let his cigarette burn. "This good enough? I wanted to screw your brains out because I fucking hate you."

She broke eye contact with him, the feeling of total embarrassment took a hold of her. There was nothing in any language she could say to that.

He hated her.

Silence etched itself into the room and neither of them spoke, only the distant dripping of a pipe.

* * *

Ian couldn't look at her anymore. He laid down on the couch and stared at the imperfections in the ceiling. Each inhale of tobacco wasn't satisfying him.

He didn't want to think about it. About any of it. Especially what it was like touching her. He had to accept the idea he could never touch her again. It was the best he ever had. Everything else felt pale in comparison.

She had moaned so devastatingly hot in his ear when she was done. He had gripped the seat because he barely came out of her in time.

"Ian?" Her voice interrupted his thoughts. "I'm losing feeling in my arms."

* * *

He stomped out his cigarette and crossed the room to her. He leaned down and untied her hands from the back and immediately raised her arms above her head and tied them back together.

She considered head butting him and making a run for it, but in a survey of the warehouse, no exit had any chance of prevailing.

"I know what you're thinking."

She glared at him. "Oh? You're telepathic now?"

"You're thinking about how you can get out of here."

"Wouldn't you be thinking that?"

He kneeled down in front of her to tie her hands to each armrest.

"For what it's worth, I don't believe you."

"Dani. I know you'll say anything to me right now. Do you think I'm stupid?"

"No. You were smart enough to trick me."

He finished tying her to one side and eagerly went to finish the other.

"You think I'm afraid of what happens to me? You think that's my end game?"

"Isn't it everyone's?"

She shook her head. A tear fell down her face she couldn't prevent. "Not mine."

"Dani—"

"What did you say about me? I'm too honest? You know I won't lie to you. It's that I don't want this for you."

He completely stopped tying the knot. "You should hate my guts, Dani. Not feel sorry for me."

"Have sex with me again."

He seemed caught off guard. "What?"

"I won't try anything. We could say goodbye. Everything's going to shit anyway."

He closed his eyes. "You know I can't do that."

"You did last night. What's the difference?"

"Because I can't!" He finally snapped.

She slowed her words. "It should be easy for you. I'm just an eight-million-dollar whore you hate."

His lip trembled.

She leaned down. "You made love to me, Ian. Not even the best liar can fake that."

Her lips touched his cheek. She expected him to flinch to her touch, but he turned his lips toward her and kissed her gently.

"What the shit is going on?"

Ian abruptly stood up when Owen walked in. "Hey man. What's up?"

Owen pointed at both of them. "What's this?"

Dani noticed Ian fidget his fingers and she remembered he left his gun on the couch.

"Nothing."

"You were kissing the bitch. That ain't nothing."

"So? I've kissed her before. It's not like it means anything."

"That's when you were tricking her. My guess is you were thinking about letting her go."

Ian was quiet one second too long prompting Owen to draw his gun.

Ian held up his hands. "No way. I ain't ditching eight mill. I was just going to have fun with her."

Owen grinned. "Alright. But I want her first."

Dani's heart sank.

Oh God, no.

Ian's reaction wasn't exactly painted on the back of his head. She didn't know what he would do.

"Whatever. I need a smoke." Ian walked out of the warehouse without bothering to turn around.

Of all the things Ian Price did to her, that pierced her heart the deepest.

Owen came over and cut the binding on her wrists. He didn't care her ribs were sore. He dragged her across the concrete and shoved her out the back. Her legs were still bound so she clenched her fists and fought him in the dark as long as she could.

This was it. Rock bottom. She had found it.

He stood over her. She couldn't see his face but she could hear him undoing his belt.

Owen was suddenly struck and dropped to the dirt.

"I'm so sorry, Dani." Ian kneeled down and raised her up. "I had to let him lower his guard."

She couldn't help it. She hit her breaking point. She started to sob uncontrollably.

He touched her hair. "God, I'm the biggest dipshit. Fuck all this. Let's get you out of here."

"Yeah, I don't think so." Clare was standing in the backdoor with a gun in her hand.

19

"WALKING ME ON A LEASH TO THE POLICE?"

"Take a good look at him."

Ian's mouth and hands were wrapped in duct tape. His face was bruised with purple and blue from Preston's beating. Dani had the front row seat of his punishment.

After Preston shot Owen in the head due to him exhausting a purpose, Dani and Ian had been tied up and separated for the last thirty-six hours.

"I want you to think about him, about Agnes, before you do anything stupid in there. You get me?"

Dani slowly turned her head and stared at the cold barrel of a gun. "Of course, I do, Clare. You're not that original."

Clare slapped the shit out of her. After stowing her pistol in her red leather jacket, she opened a tiny bag with flowers on it and smeared concealer on Dani's face to cover up something suspicious.

Clare opened the sliding van door, and the scenery of Grey Vein downtown came into view. It was jarring to see people without a care in the world walk up and down the street like everything was normal. She envied the innocent time.

She swallowed to rid gravel from her throat. She tried to remember the last time she had anything in her mouth besides spit. Her whole body ached and her head felt like it was splitting open with a meat cleaver. She thought she had known what hunger and thirst was. She had not.

"Can you move your ass?" Clare elbowed her.

Dani moved one foot in front of the other until they were in a private office at the credit union. She was relieved to sit down and not move.

"You must be the one I spoke with on the phone?" A man in a suit helped them get papers drafted so Dani could make Clare a joint owner on the account. Clare spun a story about them starting a fashion line together, when in reality, Clare would empty the account and hightail it and run, forever evading authority.

Dani stared at the white piece of paper too long because Clare dug her nails into her leg underneath the desk. "You're not having second thoughts, are you?"

She signed her name and the banker extended his hand to shake on it. "Excellent. I wish both of you the best of luck."

They stood up to leave and Dani felt the last bit of sand fall in her hourglass. She needed a miracle.

That's when she saw her. It was the deaf woman she met at the clinic. She remembered Ella mentioning working as a prison guard before she was deaf. Now apparently, she worked here. She had to get this woman's attention, and without the use of sound, no less. "Can I go to the bathroom?"

Clare looked at her like she was nuts. "Go in your pants."

"I didn't mean by myself. You can go with me."

"No."

Dani went for it. She pretended to faint. It wasn't hard. She was so dizzy and lethargic it seemed natural.

Clare immediately tried to yank her back up like she could rewind the damage. "Dani!"

The man in the suit kneeled. "Miss, are you alright?"

Dani opened one eye and saw Ella stop what she was doing. She stared at her through the glass with a look of concern. Dani didn't dare break eye contact.

Please recognize her.

While they were helping her back to her feet, Ella's eyes lit up. The curls of her hair bounced as she waved. She seemed happy to see her again, but Dani did a slight shake of her head and did sign language at her side. *S-O-S.*

"Let's go!" Clare looped her arm through hers and jerked her out the main entrance. "What was that about?"

"What? Falling over? I haven't had food or water in two days."

Clare rolled her eyes like food and water wasn't a necessity. "You almost screwed us back there."

"I wish I could I say I was sorry."

When Clare got the van door closed, she slapped her again.

Preston was still in the driver's seat, unfazed by the commotion. "Well?"

Clare was nursing her hand after hitting so hard with it. "We got it. Let's get the hell out of here."

A few blocks down the road, Dani heard the most wonderful sound in the world.

Sirens.

Thank you, Ella.

The cops drove up alongside and swerved in front of them.

"What is going on?!" Clare yelled like it was Preston's fault.

"Why are you asking me? What happened at the bank?"

Clare cocked her gun like she was about to shoot Dani, but Ian used all his body weight to kick her. Her gun went sliding across the van floor.

Preston jerked them all by slamming on the brakes.

The police got out of their cars. "This is the Grey Vein Police Department. Step outside of the vehicle with your hands behind your head!"

Preston panicked and made a run for it.

There was a lot of gunfire. Preston shot at the police giving them no choice but to shoot back. With them distracted, Clare bolted out the back.

The selfish part of Dani wanted to stay. She would already be at a disadvantage. She couldn't catch her with two days of no food, water, or sleep. Even still, miracles happened every day. A parting of the Red Sea came to mind.

Dani went out the back.

"Stop! Stop right there!" Police were yelling but she kept running.

She was counting on Clare running very little in her spare time, while Dani had routinely in a feeble attempt to tire herself out.

Clare went through a shop off the street. Dani heard the fire exit door ding in the back.

"Hey!" The shopkeeper was shouting at them.

Clare ran down an alley and turned left, tripping over some garbage bags that bought Dani a little distance. Her lungs and side were now on fire and her legs felt as if they would buckle at any moment. She kept going.

She eventually lost her, but it became clear where Clare was going. Dani reached the docks and saw countless sailboats and people filling the pier. She scanned for blonde hair and a red jacket but couldn't spot her. The crowds of people rushed by her. It was hard to scan everyone at once. She prayed for a sign, clarity in the distracting mess.

One of the yachts in the harbor bumped into another boat on departure. This had to be Clare. No one would ram another boat unless they were in too much of a hurry.

Dani ran to the closest thing she could use. She hijacked someone's jet ski, fully aware of angry people shouting obscenities at her.

It was frightening when she skidded across the water at this high of a speed. She had never been a fan of dark water, but getting thrown into it wasn't really her biggest problem anymore.

When she closed the distance, she veered to the right so Clare couldn't abruptly stop the engine and make her crash in the back end.

She revved up the jet ski. Her legs violently wobbled, and she almost lost her grip. She jumped over the railing of the boat, scraping her leg something awful.

She looked around for a weapon. There was a cooler with beer bottles in them. It was better than nothing. She grabbed one and smashed it over the metal edge when something popped her in the shoulder.

She gripped the railing to stabilize herself. Clare was holding an oxygen tank and all Dani had was half a glass bottle.

"I was aiming for your head."

"Clare. I'm not here to hurt you."

"Yeah? I want to beat your face in. I guess we're different like that."

"Clare—"

"If you had done what I told you, Preston would still be alive."

Dani took in a deep breath. She wondered if there were anything she could say to make Clare drop that canister. She wasn't off to a good start.

"Somehow, even after weeks of planning, you still managed to outsmart me. How is that even possible?"

"You should have come to me."

"What?"

"I would have given you the money."

Clare laughed at her. "Sure. Sure, you would have."

Dani didn't see anything funny about this. "I would have. I don't care about money."

"What do you care about, Dani? You're a freak show, you know that? You know how hard it was for Ian to get close to you? Good grief. Any other girl would have banged his brains out, but no, not you."

Dani looked down.

"Well. How about that. There is some human in you."

Of all emotions that could spawn in this moment it was only deep sadness that penetrated her bones. She saw this fragile child standing in front of her, a product of a fiend who'd abused her. "I'm sorry for what happened to you."

Her cousin's eyes widened.

"I know deep down you don't want to hurt anyone. You're just destitute. And not even for money, for a new life. You thought this money could do that." Dani held out her free hand. "Let me help you."

"With what? Walking me on a leash to the police?"

"No." She couldn't believe she was saying this. "I'll get you out of here."

Clare blinked at her. "Are you—are you nuts? After what I did to you?"

"Yes, Clare. After what you did to me."

"How stupid do you think I am? You think you can trick me."

"That's everyone else's thing. Not mine." Dani took a step forward, her hand still helplessly outstretched.

Clare finally snapped. She started laughing hysterically and Dani's heart shattered into a million pieces.

Without warning Clare lunged at her. Dani ducked and blocked, but the glass bottle was still in her hand. Clare immediately dropped the canister and touched her throat. The glass had sliced it open.

"Clare!"

She collapsed on the deck.

Dani took off her shirt to put pressure on it. Blood soaked through immediately, settling in a heartbreaking outcome. "It was an accident."

Her cousin grabbed her arm. Her lips made no sound, but she mouthed she was sorry.

"I know." Dani sat there for a long time holding Clare's lifeless body, too paralyzed with despair to move.

20

"I'LL BLAME YOUR BEHAVIOR ON PAINKILLERS."

Dani saw him out of the corner of her eye, a man who frequented the halls of the dead and the injured. He entered the hospital recreation room, which was filled with inhabitants passing the time with board games as their bodies healed.

His uniform was crisp, absent of a single piece of lint. His hair was neatly combed back, and his face was kissed by the sun. "Miss Poe?"

"Can it wait? I'm winning my first game of checkers."

Her opponent, as if on cue, hopped over two checker pieces and confiscated them.

"Never mind. I'm losing again."

He shifted his weight to one side, a sure sign he was losing patience with her. "The hospital has a private room we can speak in."

"Not necessary. Me and Wyleen don't keep secrets from each other."

The elderly woman across from her chuckled.

"Miss Poe, I need a moment of your time." His voice was more assertive.

"Why do I have to keep talking to you people? And why do I even have to be here?"

"You're being treated for severe dehydration from the report I read."

"Sure. And so, I've suffered the indignity of hopping across the room in a paper-thin nightgown to a toilet in front of the men in uniform."

Wyleen and a few others nearby laughed.

"I do apologize."

"I'm sure."

"I've been investigating a person of interest and I need to speak with you. I'm asking as a personal favor, not as a policeman."

She looked at Wyleen. "When I get back, I want a rematch of the rematch."

She followed him until they were in a staff break room. It was quiet apart from the continuous hum of vending machines.

"You thirsty?" he asked.

"Depends. Got any rum?"

He gave her a look.

"That was a joke, obviously."

He sat across from her. "I'll blame your behavior on painkillers."

"That's fair."

"Even though I know you're not on any." He began to claw around in a brown file folder. He set a tape recorder on the table. "State your name for the record."

"Are you serious?"

He shut the folder. Slowly his finger went for the dial on the recorder. He clicked the off switch. "Your name?"

She tilted her head in confusion. "Danitayla Poe. But you already know that. What's yours?"

He seemed surprised she wanted to know his name. "Nathan Greer."

"Alright, Nathan Greer. What can I do for you?"

He slid a photograph across the table. "I'm sure you recognize this individual."

She took a peek at the picture. It was a man standing against metric walls with a plaque stating the arrest number and county locale. He looked much younger in the picture. "Sebastian Santos."

"I want to rewind. You were the beneficiary of $8.1 million, correct?"

"This case is over. Solved. Terminado. What do you want?"

Greer scratched his head like he was perplexed but it felt artificial. "I don't understand why you're defensive."

"You'll have to forgive me for being that way."

Suddenly it felt icy cold in the room even before he said it. "I know where the money came from."

She couldn't fake a reaction on her face.

"And so do you. It's not hard for an obsessed person like me to put pieces together. I know it was from a robbery fourteen years ago. I know about Santos, your father, and uncle's setup. And just between me and you, I think Ian Price was involved."

"I have to say, I'm getting really tired of this blackmailing routine."

His mouth held the tiniest hint of satisfaction.

"I'm guessing you want the money in exchange for not pursuing obstruction of justice charges against me?"

He blinked. "You think that's what I'm after?"

"You would be an anomaly if you weren't. Everyone is after the same thing it appears."

He slowly leaned back in his chair. "You can take the money and shove it up someone's ass for all I care."

"You get more interesting by the minute."

"I arrested Santos a long time ago, me and my old partner did. Are you aware of that?"

She shook her head. "My grandmother never told me."

"That's because he got off the hook from a trial." He paused. "When I threatened him, he killed my pregnant wife."

It was naive to think Santos only killed two people and those two people were her mother and father. "I'm sorry."

"I always knew he did it." He swirled his finger on the table. "I used to follow him. I would watch him through windows drinking at cafes, buying hotdogs from a cart on the street. I'd sit there in my car and fantasize about snapping his neck with my bare hands. I was unstable back then. Even worked up the courage to kill him. He almost killed me in the process."

This man sitting across from her was a total stranger and yet he was telling her these things.

"I'm glad he's dead."

"I think I can understand that." Dani was still waiting for his reason for being there. The uneasiness she was feeling was only amplifying.

"I want to cut a deal."

"A deal."

"I say nothing to anyone about what I know."

"In exchange for what?"

"You tell me how you killed Santos."

She felt her eyebrows rise. "You want me to tell you, what, details?"

"Every single one you can think of, down to the lighting in the room. And I'm going to record it for my own sick satisfaction. Undoubtedly listen to it like an insane person in need of a straitjacket." He stretched out his hand to shake on it. "Reasonable?"

Clearly, this man was troubled. Listening to a description of his enemy's demise would not bring him peace. Maybe it would take this however for him to realize that. "This is the weirdest thing I've ever agreed to."

"Trust me. Something weirder will come." He clicked the tape recorder back on. "Life is funny like that."

* * *

"Dani?"

She opened her vision. "Grandmother?"

"You fell asleep. I didn't want to wake you, but Hazel is here."

Dani rose from the couch and rubbed her eyes.

"Bad dream?" Agnes asked.

"No. Not anymore, thank God." Through the window, Dani saw the angelic scene of neighbor kids playing fetch with a dog. The leaves around them had started turning beautiful yellow, orange, and red. It was pretty enough for a photographer's backdrop.

Dani went for the front door.

"Hi!" Hazel pulled Dani into a hundredth hug since her return home.

"How long are you going to treat me like a cancer patient?"

"You kind of went through an ordeal. Take the hugs."

"For the nine thousandth time, I'm ok." She noticed a guy in Hazel's passenger seat. "Who's that?"

"Oh, that's Jasper," Hazel beamed. "We're kind of an item now."

"Jasper from your physics class?"

"Oh, you've met him?"

"Not sober, but yes." Dani waved at him.

"He was the only one nice to me that day I was ugly. I finally have my worthy man." Hazel hugged herself.

Dani was happy for her.

"Anyway. Do you want to come with us to the mall? I thought you might want to get out of the house."

"I—ah—have something to take care of first."

Hazel didn't pry. "Ok. Some other time." She turned to leave.

Dani almost didn't say it. "Hazel."

Her friend stopped and turned.

"You know I love you, right? That you're my family?"

Hazel smiled. "Yes, Dani. I've always known that."

* * *

Dani turned into Dax Auto and shut the engine off. She touched her throat, convinced her heart had resided there. She so loathed that sensation.

With the heavy duffle bag strapped to her back, she slowly inched toward the garage. The wind and pine straw whipped at her as she neared the entrance.

She spotted two mechanics submerged in a car hood. Their heads popped out with grease painted faces. "You need something, darling?"

"Ian's not here," Brent spoke from her right.

"Hey, Brent. Where is he?"

"Said he had some errands, then he was going by your place, I thought."

"I guess I missed him."

"Well, you're welcome to wait at his cabin."

She watched Brent return to his office, oblivious of the ordeal that ensued because of him. It wasn't her place to tell him though.

She headed for the back door. In the daylight, she could appreciate the intricate details of Ian's home. A tin roof with three logs were evenly balanced for the front porch. She found solace in the wooden swing.

She looked down at Meeko who followed her. He laid down at her feet and waited with her. She listened to nature and the squeaks of a chain until Ian's motorcycle overpowered the singing amphibians. He parked next to his home and walked up the porch. He noticed her. "Dani."

She stood up.

"I just went by your house." He walked up to the door and unlocked it. "You can come in."

She didn't go in.

He nervously fisted his hands into his pockets. "I was coming to see you. To apologize mostly. And, to thank you."

"Thank me for what?"

"For not telling the cops about me." He took a step forward. "I've thought a lot about this. I don't know what could be said to make any of this shit right. Everything got so screwed up. I was. And I'm sorry."

"I forgive you." She turned and dragged the duffle bag toward him.

He leaned down and unzipped the bag. Inside were twenty-seven thousand crisp one-hundred-dollar bills.

"That was your share wasn't it? Two point seven million? I'm assuming Owen wasn't getting a cut."

He looked up. "I don't want this. What are you doing?"

"Give it to Liza, clear Brent's debt. It's what you wanted. Enough to ruin my life over it."

He stood up. "You didn't turn me in. Now you're trying to give me the money. Why?"

His black hair rustled in the wind and sunshine radiated off his gorgeous skin. It felt like his eyes could melt stars from the sky. "I didn't fall in love with you because you're beautiful. Or whatever other bullshit reason."

"I know."

"And not because you stuck up for me when Rebecca did what she did. Your offer to protect me when I traveled to Grey Vein. Or when you took me to a mountain to stare at something greater than yourself. All that was fiction anyway."

He waited.

"That's how I knew it was real. Because I loved you and there wasn't a reason."

He smiled. "I think I know how it works."

"Sure you do." It came out as cold as she felt it.

His smile faded. "You don't believe me."

"Why should I?"

It was like he came apart right in front of her. "Dani, please don't do this. You have to believe me. I only care about you."

"You had me. I gave you me in the backseat of my car and it wasn't enough. Don't you understand? People died. I killed them, because of you. Now you think we can ride off in the sunset together, nothing made right."

"I wish I could take it back, Dani." He started crying. "I would do anything to take it back. I'm not that person anymore."

"Then throw the money in a dumpster and turn yourself in."

He swallowed. "You didn't turn me in to see if I would do the right thing."

She didn't deny it.

"And you don't think I will."

She didn't deny that either. "No."

He wiped the tears from his face and pushed the duffle bag toward her with his foot. "I guess you'll just have to be wrong about me again."

*　*　*

An abandoned industrial property was the perfect place for it. Its only visitors were teenagers destroying their liver or brain, depending on the poison. Everyone knew about it but pretended it wasn't the pinnacle of Riftin's shady activities.

She dumped the stacks of one-hundred-dollar bills in the oil drum. Eight point one million.

There was something satisfying about watching it saturate as she poured gasoline over the top. Laying on a basement floor with a serrated stomach, the unnecessary death, devised manipulation, Ian Price being in jail. It was for this.

The illogical thing stitched in humans demanded she wait for him on the other side of concertina wire fence.

She lit a match and tossed it within.

And watched it burn.

CPSIA information can be obtained
at www.ICGtesting.com
Printed in the USA
LVHW080043060422
715457LV00005B/233

9 781662 920592